"Don't . . . Please, Joe," Amber Begged As Joe Reached For Her.

"You're asking the impossible," he said harshly. "I want you so badly I'm burning up inside, and you want me, too."

With a sob Amber turned away. "What either of us wants doesn't matter. My career and life-style are totally opposed to yours. We no longer belong together."

His mouth slid the collar of her robe aside, and his teeth bit gently into the vulnerable flesh between her neck and shoulder. "But do you want to become my lover again?"

"I can't," she moaned. But before she could stop him, he parted the thick fabric of her robe, and his mouth began to feast hungrily on hers.

"Aren't you willing?" he asked.

With a mindless compulsion she could no longer fight, her arms rose to circle his neck. "Oh, Joe," she said faintly. "Yes."

Dear Reader:

Happy New Year!

It takes two to tango, and we've declared 1989 as the "Year of the Man" at Silhouette Desire. We're honoring that perfect partner, the magnificent male, the one without whom there would *be* no romance. January marks the beginning of a twelve-month extravaganza spotlighting one book each month as a tribute to the Silhouette Desire hero—our *Man of the Month*!

Created by your favorite authors, you'll find these men are utterly irresistible. You'll be swept away by Diana Palmer's Mr. January (whom some might remember from a brief appearance in *Fit for a King*), and Joan Hohl's Mr. February is every woman's idea of the perfect Valentine. . . .

Don't let these men get away!

Yours,

Isabel Swift
Senior Editor & Editorial Coordinator

NICOLE MONET
Twilight over Eden

Silhouette Desire

Published by Silhouette Books New York

America's Publisher of Contemporary Romance

SILHOUETTE BOOKS
300 East 42nd St., New York, N.Y. 10017

ISBN: 0-373-05473-4

First Silhouette Books printing January 1989

All the characters in this book are fictitious. Any
resemblance to actual persons, living or dead, is
purely coincidental.

Printed in the U.S.A.

NICOLE MONET,

an inveterate writer of romance, lives in California with her husband and daughter and makes of her writing a full-time career. "I write," the author says, "because I am a voracious reader, and I feel that in some small way, I'm paying back all the pleasure I've received in my lifetime."

One

Joseph Morrow entered the lobby of the glitzy Reno hotel where he was registered, his hand resting possessively against a softly curved, very feminine hip. As a man, he could appreciate the slick feel of satin against his palm and the heat from the body it covered. It had been a long time since he'd been with a woman—a very long time. The cloyingly sweet scent of his companion's perfume rose to his nostrils, but he ignored the momentary pang of distaste that rippled through him.

He tightened his grip over the pants that hugged her figure like a second skin and reassured himself that Sally's fragrance of choice wasn't important. All that mattered was that Sally was an amusing companion, and he was in the mood to be amused.

The name didn't sound right and he frowned. He never should have had that second double Scotch, but he'd been preoccupied by the winsome Sally—or was it Suzie? Damn, it was hot in here! Joe shook his head to clear it and sucked in a deep breath. The spinning room settled a bit, although multicolored prisms from one of the huge crystal chandeliers overhead seemed to ricochet off his aching eyeballs.

His gait became steadier as they crossed the garishly red- and gold-carpeted foyer in the direction of the elevators, and his alcohol-fogged mind cleared enough from the exercise for him to remember his informal introduction to his date for the evening. Her name was Stella, he recalled with a relieved sigh. Stella of the tight pants and low-cut blouse, who had waited on him as he'd been killing time in a restaurant down the street.

As one hour had dragged into two her smile had become more inviting, her manner teasingly provocative. Joe knew that his appearance attracted women. They seemed partial to his black hair and eyes and his lean, muscular body. It was something he took for granted, in the same way he did his good health, even his white teeth and athletic grace of movement.

Downplaying his looks was a habit retained from childhood, since his formative years had been spent fighting anyone who dared to call him "pretty boy." Even his younger brothers, Adam and Paul, had been given a taste of his fists upon occasion, although usually members of the Morrow clan were known for their protective attitude toward each other. Still, being the eldest of five kids had been no picnic, especially since he was the only one to take after his beautiful Italian mother in looks.

Although he was nearly as tall as Joe, Adam had his father's golden-brown hair and eyes. Little brother Paul had Pop's coloring as well as his shorter, stockier build and Paula was a more feminine version of her twin. Aileen, the baby of the family, was a one-off—she'd inherited her paternal grandmother's violet-blue Irish eyes and brown-streaked blond hair. He smiled at the thought of Pop cheerfully taking sole credit for his youngest daughter's loveliness, much to his mother's annoyance.

His grin slowly faded as the brief mental foray into the past brought about a familiar sense of isolation. For too long he had neglected that special bonding with his family. When the woman he loved had walked out on him, Joe had closed himself off from the rest of humanity like an animal in pain. His brother Adam, who had lost his little girl Gail to muscular dystrophy, had come closest to understanding the raw, aching loneliness in Joe's soul.

But even Adam hadn't been able to prevent the hardening of Joe's spirit that had accompanied Amber's defection. He winced as the name reverberated in his mind, the echo both a prayer and a curse. A harsh, almost silent laugh rumbled in his chest. He prayed he'd never be taken in like that by another woman and cursed the day he'd ever become captivated by a pair of glowing emerald eyes.

Joe no longer gave a damn about much of anything except his career, and that cynical single-mindedness had been his downfall as a member of the Los Angeles Police Department. Working undercover in the streets to help clean up some of the human scum littering the city had given his life meaning and purpose again, but he had taken too many risks and been involved in too many dangerous assignments. It had gotten him noticed by his superiors in a way he hadn't counted on.

Joe ground his teeth in frustration at the thought. He'd turned down a promotion that would have placed him primarily behind a desk. To give him time to reconsider, the powers-that-be had ordered him off duty for two months. Just because he didn't view the world through rose-colored glasses he'd been judged and found wanting, Joe thought angrily. If he'd become hard and disillusioned over the past few years, he figured he was a better cop because of it. Unfortunately his superiors didn't share his point of view.

Although he'd been tempted to argue with them, a saner, more logical part of his brain had taken over.

As much as he hated to admit it, he was mentally and physically exhausted. In his line of work, that kind of stress could get a man killed. So he'd decided to spend some time in Nevada enjoying wine, women and song. Joe sighed heavily and glanced around him with indifference. Well, he was here in Reno, he'd had enough booze to make him glow like a firefly, he could hear rock music from the Cabaret Lounge in the distance and there was an attractive woman by his side. The only trouble was, he still didn't give a damn.

Adam had argued that it was rest he needed and had given him the key to his vacation cabin. "Coloma's not far from Reno," Adam had informed him, "and you'll enjoy the fishing. With Beth's delivery date so close, we'll have to wait until the baby's born before we can do much traveling."

Joe felt a recurrence of the swift stab of envy he'd experienced at his brother's words and quickly shoved the memory to the back of his mind. Glancing down at the impossibly silver curls on the woman's head resting against his shoulder, he noticed the dark roots emerging from his companion's scalp. Far from putting him off, the sight caused him to feel pleased with his choice of diversion for the evening. Blonde or brunette, he didn't give a damn—as long as her hair wasn't tinted with the fire of a dawn sky.

"Hey, that hurts!"

Stella's reproachful voice drew Joe from the blackness of his thoughts, and his heart was pounding against his rib cage as though he'd just awakened from a nightmare. It took him a moment to register her complaint, and another to realize his fingers were gripping her hip with bruising force. Giving her a repentant look, he shifted his hand to her waist. "Sorry, honey. My mind was miles away."

Stella's smile held uncertainty. "That's not very flattering."

Joe wasn't in the mood to pander to her injured ego, but he wasn't averse to using diversionary tactics. With as much enthusiasm as he could muster, he said, "The evening's still young, gorgeous. How about giving lady luck a whirl for a couple of hours?"

He could tell by the anticipation in her eyes that all was forgiven, and he guided her toward the steps leading down into the casino area of the huge hotel. Immediately they were surrounded by the almost frenetic movements of the people around them. For the first time Joe noticed how stale and artificial the air smelled, and the garish lighting caused him to narrow his eyelids in discomfort.

But it was the noise around him that was the biggest irritant to his ragged nerves. Pinging bells, coins dropping against metal trays, the muted roar of voices, the discordant sound of excited screams and half-hysterical laughter. He suddenly wondered what the hell he was doing here when he could be enjoying the peace and tranquility of Adam's cabin.

Stella stopped in front of a dollar slot machine and turned to nudge his chest with her shoulder. "How about it, darlin'?"

Barely preventing himself from flinching at the endearment, Joe schooled his expression into one of bland neutrality. The back of his neck was beginning to ache, a portent of one of the vicious migraines that had been plaguing him for months. Wordlessly he hailed a black- and white-uniformed woman wearing a heavy change belt and slipped her a fifty dollar bill. With a look of bored indifference she dropped a handful of brown, paper-wrapped coins into his open palm, her automatic smile and murmured well wishes as false as her eyelashes.

A noxious odor was drifting toward them from the cigar of a fleshy jowled man on their right, and after placing his money in Stella's hands Joe automatically stepped back to avoid the stream of smoke. Stella, he noticed, seemed oblivious to any discomfort. She was also, he realized with a good deal of chagrined amusement, oblivious to him.

Joe refused to give in to the sudden feeling of exhaustion sweeping over him, and his eyes scanned the room with a lack of interest he found frustrating. He felt strangely unsettled, almost disassociated with the movements of the people around him. His gaze became fixed on the spinning roulette wheel a few yards away. That was the way he felt, as though his mind was revolving around and around without purpose or direction.

Although it didn't take long for the slot machine to eat his money, by the time he and Stella wandered toward the blackjack tables boredom seemed firmly cemented into Joe's skull, and he was annoyed with his own irrational changeability. What in the hell was the matter with him? he wondered irritably. Now that the effects of the alcohol he'd consumed earlier were wearing off, he was as jumpy as a cat on hot bricks.

When a single space opened at the crowded blackjack table, Joe pushed Stella forward with a relieved smile. "You go ahead and play, honey. I'm not feeling particularly lucky right now."

She glanced at him over her shoulder, tiny frown lines appearing between her brows. "Are you sure, Joe? We can leave if you want."

Although his nod was abrupt, she seemed reassured. After buying a stack of chips and placing them in front of her, Joe stepped back from the press of bodies. He felt stifled by the warm atmosphere and when a yawn took him by surprise, he wondered wryly if he was getting old. Right now he felt like thirty-two going on eighty.

He turned, stretching restlessly, and suddenly every sane thought left his head. A woman was standing a few yards away, four tuxedo-clad men by her side. She was adorned in a clinging, silky black sheath dress that showed every curve of her body to full advantage. His gaze slid up a deliciously long pair of legs and a svelte, naked back with skin as white and smooth as a porcelain figurine.

Stiffening in disbelief, he realized why Amber had been so much on his mind this evening. He'd always been able to sense her presence before she walked into a room. Anguish exploded inside him at the realization that nothing had really changed since he'd last seen her. He let his gaze follow the line of her long, elegantly shaped neck. Her head was tilted at an imperious angle, her manner distant as she spoke to the men beside her.

Joe swallowed sickly, his throat tightening as he noticed how even the severity of the stylish French braid she wore failed to subdue the color of her hair. It was a rich, glorious shade of red . . . a red as vibrant and unforgettable as a sunrise. One bare, delicate arm lifted and she pointed across the room. The men at her side immediately walked away to enter a nearby change booth, but Joe was so intent on studying Amber that he hardly noticed their departure.

Amber Stevenson watched the men leave with a feeling of relief. She hated the two nights a week she set apart for her inspection of the casino floor, especially since those evenings were usually added to a full day in the upstairs office. Tonight had been no

different, and she felt weighted down with tiredness.
She glanced at the gold bracelet watch on her wrist
and grimaced when she noticed it was nearly eleven
o'clock. She hadn't slept last night, and her body was
feeling much the worse for wear. Although she'd
spent a couple of hours lying down after dinner, it
had been a wasted effort. She'd been too keyed up to
sleep.

The recurrent bouts of insomnia were happening
more frequently, she realized. What she needed was
time away from work to relax—something she
avoided like the plague. Unless she exhausted herself during the day, her nights were long and rest-
less. Work was a panacea she needed to function,
and she had no intention of giving it up, even temporarily.

Theo had been warning her about the necessity for
delegating authority, and she pressed her lips together with annoyance as she remembered one more
in a long series of arguments between them. "There's
no need for you to work yourself to death," he'd
roared in his indomitable fashion, but as usual she
hadn't paid much attention. He might own this
casino, as well as a good portion of Las Vegas, she
thought, but he didn't own her!

With a familiar sensation of futility, she wondered why most of their conversations developed into
arguments. Theo was as stubborn and strong-willed
as she was, but when she'd agreed to work for him it

had been with the understanding that after a minimal training period she would be the one fully in charge of managing the casino.

Since he'd wanted her with him he had agreed, and on a production level he was satisfied with her efforts. It was on a personal level where their difficulties arose. As far as she was concerned he had no say over her private life and never would have. He had relinquished any rights over her a long time ago.

A stray wisp had escaped from her tightly bound hair, and she brushed it from her cheek with annoyance. This was her last stop of the evening, and for once she'd decided to let her assistants handle the final tally. She pushed aside a momentary feeling of guilt, her mind centered on the hot, scented tub of water she planned to soak in when she returned to her suite. Usually she made do with a quick shower, but tonight she was going to wallow in the luxury of spending a little extra time on herself.

When she had moved to Reno, Theo had wanted her to share his penthouse apartment, but she had insisted on living separately. Considering how strained their relationship had become, she was glad she'd insisted on keeping her independence. Although Amber knew he cared for her in his own way, just the thought of surrendering her entire existence to Theo Carvalho made her shudder. It was bad enough being followed around by the two bodyguards he'd assigned to her over her protests, with-

out the added pressure of constantly having to
explain her comings and goings.

Amber's resentful thoughts added to her restlessness, and she pivoted on her spiked heels. This sudden urge to flee from the claustrophobic atmosphere
of the casino wasn't a new one, but she had long ago
accepted the fact that for her there was no real escape. Even if she left Reno, she would never be released from Theo's protection. If he had one
weakness, she decided sadly, it was his fear of having the people he cared about become a target for
terrorists.

Theo was a very insecure man. Considering the
tragedies he'd suffered during his lifetime, she
couldn't blame him for having become paranoid
about maintaining a rigid security system. What she
did blame him for was making her a part of it. She
didn't like having her freedom curtailed, and although the men he'd assigned to see to her safety
were for the most part unobtrusive, just knowing
they were watching her was a constant irritant.

As she began walking across the carpeted floor,
Amber paid little attention to her surroundings. She
had become adept at withdrawing into herself, which
was the only way she could enjoy any peace of mind.
She had always felt shy and awkward in large gath-
erings, and that uneasiness had intensified over the
past few years. The smile that suddenly curved her
lips held no amusement, only wry acknowledge-

ment. If she wasn't careful, she decided, she was going to become as personally isolated from the rest of humanity as Theo was.

She didn't know exactly when she sensed that she was being stared at, but she began anxiously studying the people surging around her. Suddenly she stumbled to a halt, one face jumping out at her with a shock that made her gasp aloud. Instantly she was catapulted into the past, her lips automatically forming a single name.

As if drawn by her silent call, Joe began to move toward her—his approach as slow and sinuous as a panther stalking its prey. It was an excellent comparison, she decided half-hysterically, her entire body tightening in protest at the leashed anger in his piercing black eyes.

"It's been a long time, Amber."

Her indrawn breath was audible, and her voice shook like an aspen in the wind as she whispered, "Hello, Joe. How have you been?"

His mouth formed a cynical curve at the banality of her question. "Fine, and I can see you've been even better."

Amber flinched at his sarcasm, but her chin lifted in an unconscious attitude of pride. "How are Ma and Pop and the rest of the family?"

"Do you really care?" he asked harshly.

Amber flushed and lowered her eyes to the charcoal and red tie knotted at his throat. The jacket of

his gray suit was pushed back, held there by the
hands he'd slipped into his trouser pockets. His
shoulders were even broader than she remembered,
his stomach flat, his thighs bulging with muscle. Her
mouth went dry as she stared at him with the fascination of a doe caught in the glare of approaching
headlights. Realizing she was just as susceptible to his
overt masculinity as she'd ever been left her feeling
gauche, uncomfortable and very much at a disad-
vantage.

Moistening her lips with the tip of her tongue, she
replied with quiet sincerity. "Yes, I really care."

Angered by his fascination with the movements of
that little pink tongue, Joe rasped, "They're fine
now, although Ma and Pop were pretty devastated
when you took off without saying goodbye to them."

Joe had wanted to hurt her, and he knew he'd
succeeded when the flush on her cheeks faded to a
noticeable pallor. Instead of pleasure at scoring off
of her, though, he felt a guilt that made his low tones
curt and harsh when he asked, "What are you doing
in Reno?"

"I live here."

His brow arched quizzically. "Have you become
addicted to gambling?"

"No." She continued to gaze at him, her features
holding little expression. "This is where I work."

With deliberate insolence, Joe allowed his glance
to encompass her body from her black heels to the

top of her burnished hair. She had always been thin, but now her frame seemed almost heartbreakingly delicate. A swift stab of concern made him furious with himself. Why should her fragile appearance worry him? he wondered despairingly. He had stopped caring for her years ago, hadn't he? Awareness nearly stopped his heart as he sought to bury that question in his mind, while a desperate sense of self-preservation had him struggling to remind himself that there was nothing left of the relationship they'd once shared.

"You surprise me," he snarled defensively. "I didn't think you'd have to work, or at least not in a casino."

Amber bit her lip, ignoring his goading taunt. "I enjoy having a career."

"I remember when all you said you wanted was a home and children, but the idea of being married to me never really fit into your plans for the future, did it? Selling yourself to the highest bidder became a much more attractive prospect than spending your life struggling to make ends meet on a cop's salary."

Amber made a strangled sound in her throat, her eyes flashing with anger as she looked at him. "I've worked hard for everything I have, no matter what you choose to think!"

"From the looks of you, your... career is very lucrative."

Joe's eyes slid over her attire and his mouth twisted
with subdued rage. Who was she trying to kid? he
asked himself. She might be on the verge of emacia-
tion, but to all outward purposes Amber had done
very well for herself. No longer was her body clad in
well-worn jeans or simple skirts. The jewelry she
wore at wrist, neck and ears was probably insured for
a mint, and her gown bore the understated elegance
of a designer creation. She was the essence of so-
phistication, her tall, willowy frame model perfect.

No matter what she said, the simple truth was that
what he'd had to offer hadn't been enough for her.
His teeth were clenched so tightly his jaw began to
ache, and Joe briefly closed his eyes to shut out her
image. When his lashes lifted, he'd hardened his
features into a cold, impassive mask. His initial
shock at seeing Amber was wearing off, and he was
grateful for the numbness that surrounded his emotions like a protective shield.

Joe didn't want to spend any more time in Amber's company than was necessary, but he couldn't
seem to make his feet obey the dictates of his brain.
With unwilling intensity he studied the delicately
sculpted cheekbones beneath skin as smooth and
creamy as alabaster. But warm, he remembered, the
hands hidden in his pockets curling into fists...so
very warm to the touch. Her mouth looked as soft
and velvety as a perfect rosebud, its pouting fullness
tempting a man's tongue to taste and explore. His

gaze became riveted by that mouth, and the desire that slammed into his gut made him tense with resentment.

Amber withstood Joe's inspection with as much presence of mind as she could muster. Her only solace was in knowing that the conclusions he'd drawn about her were false. With a look of entreaty, she shook her head and asked stiltedly, "What about you, Joe? Have you been promoted to detective?"

Joe ignored her question, bitterness eating at his insides like bile. "What's the matter, baby? Didn't your Sugar Daddy come up to expectations? Whenever I've thought about you I pictured you at a resort for the idle rich somewhere, lazing on a nude beach while your elderly lover played shuffleboard. He is an old man, isn't he? My neighbors thrived on gossip for weeks, but I must admit they seemed more impressed with the limo he arrived in than with the guy you left me for."

"Don't, Joe," she gasped, lifting one hand as if to ward off a blow. "Please don't say anymore."

"Or maybe on a yacht, cruising around the playgrounds of the world," he interrupted with a sneer. "Tell me, was he good, Amber? Did he give you the kind of loving we shared? But it never was love, was it Amber?"

Joe began to shake as he remembered the first time Amber had shared his bed, her lovely hair spread like rippling silk over his pillow. Her initial shyness had given way to loving abandon, but the love had been all in his imagination. He deliberately blocked the memory, reminding himself of how willing a victim he'd been. It was her deceit he had to remember. Once she had made him believe that her heart was as pure as her virginal body, but subsequent events had proved him wrong. He wouldn't be taken in a second time.

"Oh, God!" Amber was tormented by his cruelty. Stricken, she began to back away from him.

"We used to get turned on just looking at each other," he continued unrelentingly. "Did that old man have the same effect on you, baby?"

Joe reached out and grabbed her, his attitude menacing as his fingers dug into the soft skin of her upper arms. "Tell me, did he dump you the way you did me? Did he give you a little of your own back? God, I hope so!"

Amber tore her eyes away from his brooding features, unable to respond to his vicious accusations. When his fingers tightened threateningly she felt no pain but a curious detachment from what was happening. She compared his tanned flesh with the whiteness of her own, the stark contrast seeming to enhance their differences. The imprint of his fingers would linger for days to remind her of this moment, she realized, but it didn't matter. Nothing mattered anymore, she thought dully, since she knew the wound he'd just inflicted on her heart would never heal. It would remain forever, a constant reminder of how much Joe hated her.

Two

—

Amber shivered convulsively, and her legs were so weak that her body began to sway. Slowly her lashes lifted, and what she saw in Joe's eyes tore at her with the sharpness of a knife blade. There was bitterness and anger there, but underlying everything was a wealth of anguish that found its mate in her. Blinking to hold back her tears, she choked, "Joe, you don't understand."

"No, I never understood how you could throw away what we had," he snapped, his eyes dark with barely banked rage. "I still don't, not that you give a damn."

"Is there a problem, Ms. Stevenson?"

The man who spoke was short and stocky but powerfully built. His dirty blond hair was swept back in a nondescript style, his clothing casual and well-suited to his surroundings. Neither he nor his companion, who was tall and lanky, would stand out in a crowd. Amber had known them long enough to realize how hard they worked at blending into their surroundings, and with a swift glance at Joe she said, "There's nothing wrong, Ray."

Ray tilted his chin pugnaciously, his steely gray eyes never leaving Joe's scowling features. "Are you sure, Ms. Stevenson?"

With a brittle smile Amber disengaged herself from Joe's clasp and turned to face the two men. She stepped back until she was standing beside Joe, and with a pointed glance at Ray and Bill she slipped her hand into the crook of his elbow. "Of course I am," she reaffirmed, feeling herself begin to tremble as her breast absorbed the heat from Joe's muscled forearm.

"This is Joseph Morrow, an old friend of mine. You two have something in common." Amber knew she was blathering like an idiot, but nervousness seemed to have taken over her tongue. Taking a steadying breath, she added, "Joe's with the LAPD."

Amber's eyes traveled from one man to the other, noticing the suspicious coldness in all three faces.

Clearing her throat, she asked, "That's where you got your initial training, isn't it, Ray?"

"Yeah," he replied, some of the hardness disappearing from his eyes as he gestured toward his partner. "I'm Ray Pierce and this is Bill Fletcher, Mr. Morrow. We hope there are no hard feelings, but we were just doing our job. From where we stood it appeared that Ms. Stevenson might be in some difficulty."

Joe nodded as he held his hand out to Ray, and Amber marveled at the charm he exuded without even trying. With deceptive casualness he disengaged his arm from hers, taking full advantage of their closeness to clasp her around her narrow waist. Amber stiffened when his mouth brushed against her temple, and she found herself resenting his self-control when his mouth curved in an indulgent expression. What disturbed her most was the knowledge that his actions were pure fabrication— not that her two bodyguards noticed.

That both Ray and Bill were taken in by his affectionate manner toward her was obvious, since both had somewhat uneasy grins on their faces. Only she was aware of the warning implicit in Joe's dark eyes, and the way his fingers dug cruelly into her flesh just a split second before he raised his head to say, "Pleased to meet you, and the name is Joe."

"We're sorry we disturbed your conversation." The sentiment was offered by Bill, in a deep, gravelly voice oddly unsuited to his thin frame. "Ray and I will leave you and Ms. Stevenson to get reacquainted in privacy."

The two seemed to dissolve into thin air as silently as they'd arrived, but Joe knew better. With an incredulous lift of his eyebrows, he muttered, "Are bodyguards really necessary?"

"Theo seems to think they are."

"Theo?" he questioned dangerously.

Stiffening her spine, Amber twisted away from the arm that still circled her like a vise. Turning slowly, she faced Joe with a composed manner that made a mockery of her inner turmoil. "Yes," she murmured faintly. "He's the man who brought me to Reno, Joe."

"So you're still together?" he responded hollowly.

"You could say that." Breathing unsteadily, her head jerked an affirmative. When she saw the disgust in his eyes it was all she could do to swallow past the lump of misery in her throat, but Amber was careful to hide her anguish. Her heart was pounding with dread, her pale features tightly controlled as she stammered, "A-and you, Joe? I...are you married, or engaged, or...or anything?"

Her teeth bit down on her bottom lip, and the small sign of discomposure gave Joe a degree of confidence that held an edge of savagery. Discovering that her lover was still a part of Amber's life was a crippling blow, and only now did he acknowledge the jealousy tearing through him.

But to be jealous a man had to care! How could he still give a damn, he asked himself incredulously, when she'd taken the very best of him with her when she left? Dear Lord, was it possible to both love and hate someone with equal intensity? His stomach muscles clenched with a wave of pain, his narrow gaze unrelenting as he surveyed the woman who had torn his life to shreds. Her professions of love had been an inbred deceit, used to keep him enslaved like any other besotted idiot who imagines that love is more than a figment of the imagination and a hunger of the flesh.

Why, then, had he never been able to accept the end of their relationship? he questioned silently. Amber had drained him of all the goodness in his soul, and now the man who had risen from that devastation was heading for another fall. The knowledge demanded payment in kind, and his voice was an outraged snarl as he responded to her question. "What business is it of yours?"

Amber winced, but managed to maintain a calm that infuriated him. "I've always wanted you to be happy, Joe."

"So much so that you left me for another man?"

"What I did was as much for you as for myself," she murmured, neither agreeing nor disagreeing with his accusation. Her hands were clasped tightly together in front of her, the rigidity of her stance betraying suppressed emotion. "I never wanted to hurt you, and surely it was better to discover we weren't suited before marriage rather than after."

"We weren't *suited*," he snorted sarcastically. "Why don't you just tell me the truth—that you wanted all the good things in life I couldn't afford to give you."

"That's not true!"

He sucked in his breath at the adamant denial, crucifying himself with sudden hope. He forced himself to speak quietly, when he longed to shout his question. "Then why did you leave me, Amber? I thought we were happy together. Was it all a lie?"

"I can't explain," she cried, tears falling onto her cheeks as she shook her head, "but I had no choice, Joe."

"We always have choices, Amber," he insisted. "Where in the hell did I fail you?"

"You didn't fail me," she murmured. "Please believe that, if nothing else, and try to forgive me if you can."

Suddenly Stella appeared at Joe's side, her expression concerned as she grasped his hand and leaned against his side. "Is something wrong, Joe?"

"Not a thing, honey," Joe murmured cynically, relieved enough by the distraction she provided to give her an indulgent smile. "Not a damn thing now that you're here."

His inference was deliberate, and as he spoke he glanced toward Amber with a challenge on his face she couldn't meet. He felt triumphant at the quickly veiled desolation in the eyes that locked with his. For a brief moment as she looked from him to Stella her expression was unguarded. In that instant Joe knew that the sensual chemistry between them was as strong as ever and that it could and would be used to his advantage.

With a muffled sob Amber turned and ran, and Joe stared after her departing figure with a heart that was bleeding from a fresh wound. She was leaving him, and for a moment he felt a sense of panic that threatened to overcome his common sense. The urge to run after her was so strong that he was humiliated by his own lack of control, and only Stella's restraining grip kept him from giving in to the crazy impulse.

Suddenly grateful to the other woman, he murmured, "I'm sorry I used you like that, Stel."

Stella didn't seem to hear his apology. She was still staring after Amber, conflicting emotions chasing across her mobile features. "God, Joe," she finally whispered on a shaky breath, "you certainly believe in living dangerously."

He whipped his head around to look at her. "What are you talking about?"

Stella jumped at the banked threat in his voice and evaded his question. "Are you still going to take me for a meal?"

It was the last thing he felt like doing. Just the thought of food was enough to cause his stomach to heave in protest. But he didn't want to be alone, not now, not when his mind was filled with confusion and his heart with despair. Three years ago Amber had woven herself into the very fabric of his existence, and she'd left too many broken threads hanging when she'd left. Now he was being split in two, the old Joe needing and wanting what he'd lost and the new Joe hating the ties that still bound him.

With instinctive knowledge he realized that if he ever hoped to be whole again, he had to escape from the seductive coils Amber had wrapped around him so long ago. She had to be exorcised from his heart and mind, and there was only one way to accomplish it. A hungry man would kill for sustenance, he thought, but wasn't one who had gorged himself at a banquet indifferent to food?

Joe thought of his brother's cozy, isolated vacation cabin, and his eyes narrowed in contemplation. If he could convince Amber to go there with him they would be completely alone, and he was certain he would be able to get her out of his system once and for all. Was there a better way to be revenged for the past, he asked himself, than by giving her a small example of what he had suffered?

This time he would be the one to sever the chains that still bound him. Amber would go with him. For all of her confident, self-assured elegance, there had been hunger in her eyes when she'd looked at him. Although a simple cabin on the banks of a river probably wasn't her ideal choice for a vacation spot, he would bet his last dollar that she was still as physically drawn to him as she'd ever been. That moment of sensual awareness had been interrupted by Stella's arrival . . . but it had been there. *Oh, yes,* he decided with certainty, *it had been there.*

He would do anything necessary to gain his own ends. He would play the cards as they were dealt, and he would satiate himself with her beautiful body. He would take her until his hunger was appeased.

But sexual satisfaction wouldn't be enough, he realized suddenly. Just once more he wanted to hear her say she loved him. Then he would turn and walk away. And never look back.

Joe shuddered inwardly at the cold calculation of his thoughts, but self-disgust didn't lessen his desire for revenge. He was the man she'd made him, and if she suffered a tenth of the agonies he had, then justice would be served. He would only be using her the way she'd used him, he argued with his conscience.

What he couldn't deal with was the knowledge that her defection had sliced through the very fabric of his existence, leaving a ragged tear that had never been mended. By spending a few weeks with her and learning to know the woman she really was, maybe he could finally rid himself of the false image he had carried around in his heart for so long.

Only then would he be free to make a future for himself without constantly looking over his shoulder at the past. God, what he wouldn't give to escape from this obsessive preoccupation that hadn't ceased to torment him from the moment she'd walked out on him!

Joe's craving for retribution was like the promise of spring after a harsh winter, and a sardonic laugh rumbled from his chest. A feeling of confidence surged through him, and for a moment a dark flame flickered within him. He remembered how Amber had been sweet wildfire in his arms, burning an imprint of her body into his flesh and mind like a brand of possession. Only now, he thought exultantly, he could enjoy the pleasure without the pain.

"Come on," he told Stella abruptly. "Let's cash in your winnings and get out of here."

Joe set his mouth in grim determination as he started guiding her around the tables. Although she followed in his wake without attempting to question him, Joe could tell that her curiosity was aroused. She slanted frowning glances in his direction as they paused briefly by a change booth, but it was only when they reached the cluster of restaurants located

opposite the reception area that she attempted to
dispel the tension that had arisen between them.

"Do you have any preferences in food?" she
asked.

Joe gave an indifferent shrug. "Anything is fine
with me."

Suddenly angry, Stella halted and grabbed at his
arm. "Look, it you don't want me around anymore
just say so!"

Joe rubbed at the tight knot which had formed at
the base of his neck. "I'm sorry," he muttered
tiredly. "I'm not very good company right now,
Stella."

"That doesn't matter," she muttered impatiently.
"I know when a man loses interest, but I can still be
a good friend when the occasion arises, Joe." She
grinned, her momentary ill humor forgotten as she
gave the traditional Boy Scout salute. "No strings, I
promise. After what I witnessed back there, it's obvious I'm out of the running. Phew! There was so
much sexual tension zinging between you two I was
tempted to duck."

Though displeased at the conclusions Stella had
drawn from his encounter with Amber, Joe was
touched by her sincere offer of friendship. But when
he opened his mouth the only words that emerged
were trite and off-putting. "You're imagining things,
Stella. I think that last Scotch went to your head."

She glared up at him with a semblance of dignity. "I switched to coffee while I was playing blackjack, and don't try to change the subject. I only butted in on you and Ms. Stevenson because it seemed as though you might need rescuing."

"You know her?" he asked quickly.

Stella gave him a searching look. "I've seen her around, but what I'd like to know is how you managed to meet her. I nearly swallowed my tongue when I saw the company you were keeping. You looked like you'd seen a ghost, which was why I rushed over as soon as those two guys left."

"Maybe because I had just seen one," he admitted wryly. "A redhead with a cash register for a heart."

Stella walked beside him, her expression thoughtful. "You didn't just meet her tonight, did you?"

"No," he admitted stiltedly, unwilling to explain further.

But Stella persisted. "Were you lovers?"

"She was my fiancée," he bit out roughly.

"Then there are some things you should know, but I'm almost afraid to tell you."

"About Amber?"

Stella nodded, her features reflecting both worry and indecision. Finally she said gently, "It doesn't pay to dredge up the past, Joe. Whatever Amber Stevenson once was to you should be forgotten—for your good, as well as her own. You'd do well to think twice before becoming involved with her again."

"That sounds like a warning," he uttered coldly. "Tell me what you know, Stella."

She jumped at the harsh inflection in his voice and glanced at him uncertainly. "I know that the lady has certain...commitments it wouldn't pay her to ignore."

Joe's smile was mocking. "Maybe she's bored and ready for a little diversion."

"There's been no evidence of that so far," she muttered in annoyance. "They don't call her the Ice Princess for nothing."

"Who doesn't?" he urged, when she fell silent.

Stella shrugged and evaded his eyes. "She manages this place. A good friend of mine is a secretary in the main office, and she's mentioned Ms. Stevenson a few times."

Joe wrapped steely fingers around her arm and studied her expressive features. "Why are you so uneasy all of a sudden? Is there something you're not telling me?"

"You're hurting me," she whispered.

Joe instantly released her and uttered a muffled curse. The conflicting emotions seething inside him were no fault of Stella's, and harassing her would serve no useful purpose. Taking a deep breath, he forced himself to relax. "I owe you another apology. I don't usually employ strong-arm tactics with a woman.''

''But you were right, Joe,'' she admitted guiltily, her eyes holding an expression very close to pity. ''There is something I'm not telling you.''

''Then we can talk in a civilized manner over a meal.'' With brusque gentleness he placed his hand against her back and urged her forward. ''It's nearly eleven o'clock, and you must be starved.''

Stella hesitated. ''Would you rather go after her, Joe? I understand she's not an easy woman to see. Usually she's surrounded by enough security to rival Fort Knox, and you'd need a cavalry brigade to even come close.''

He smiled wryly. ''I've already had a taste of that.''

Her eyes widened, as they began to walk toward one of the less formal restaurants lining the foyer. ''You mean those men I saw you talking to were...?''

''Bodyguards,'' he responded grimly, ''and don't worry. I have no intention of seeing Amber again until I've learned more about the setup here. I've already made enough of a fool of myself for one evening.''

She gave him an exasperated stare. ''I hope you can take the frustration, Joe. Right now you look like you're ready to explode.''

Joe was amused by her bluntness, and the affectionate grin he gave her was sincere and spontaneous. "You're quite a gal, do you know that?"

"Yeah." She gave a disgruntled sigh and grimaced. "That's what they all say."

"Then 'they' would be right."

Stella tilted her head to the side, a contemplative smile curving her mouth. "But you were never really interested in me, or I miss my guess."

Joe glanced at the carpet uneasily. "Stel, it's not that. You're a fantastic woman, very appealing and desirable, but I . . ."

"No need to conk me over the noggin with a sledgehammer, lover." She gave a disdainful sniff, but spoiled the haughty effect with a giggle. "You're a real prince, Joe. It's not your fault the slipper doesn't fit."

"Right now I feel more like the troll hiding in waiting for the Three Billy Goats Gruff," he admitted with embarrassed candor. "I've behaved like a jerk with you, and you have my permission to damage both of my shinbones if it'll make you feel any better."

"No harm done," she retorted cheerfully. "I've made a new friend, haven't I?"

Joe gave her a warm smile. "If you'll have me."

"A friend in hand is better than a one-night stand," she quipped with exaggerated primness, looking smugly satisfied when he gave a husky laugh.

"You're a clever lady," he said, his smile lingering. "A bit mouthy, but smart."

"Finding someone to appreciate my finer qualities is wonderful." Stella fluttered her eyelashes at him, and gave an exaggeratedly fulsome sigh. "I sure know how to pick 'em!"

Although he realized she was using flattery to try to tease him into a lighter frame of mind, Joe was quick to disagree. "You'd have been a lot better off if I'd chosen another restaurant to do my eating in."

Stella's voice held a pensive note when she said, "Don't be so hard on yourself, Joe. You're an all-right guy, and after thirty-six years of living I've tangled with enough of the other kind to know. Until you saw your ghost you weren't doing too badly."

Joe swallowed hard, dismayed at how easily she saw through him. Hoping he wasn't giving anything else away, he said, "I'm glad you don't think I'm a total washout. You're certainly good for a man's ego."

Stella stared at him in silence for a few seconds, her eyes searching his face with unconcealed compassion. "And your ego's been damaged pretty badly in the past, hasn't it? The Ice Princess, Joe?"

There was more to this woman than first met the eye, and the idea that she was perceptive enough to penetrate to the core of his emotions disturbed Joe. He'd held himself apart from other people for too long to easily relinquish his shield of aloofness. By

now they had reached the restaurant, and he was relieved to be able to divert Stella's attention by gesturing toward the line of people waiting to be seated.
"No wonder this place is open twenty-four hours. I
don't think anyone sleeps in this town."

"Oh, it'll slow down around three in the morning, although the casinos do a rousing business
around the clock. This is a tourist town, after all.
Me, I'm a country girl from Minnesota, and it was a
little difficult to get used to such a different life-style
at first. In the small town where I grew up, a big
night out consisted of drinking beer and playing
pool. But sometimes I miss it, you know?"

Joe nodded, wondering if Stella wouldn't have
been better off staying in Minnesota. He sensed she
was another of love's victims, shielding her inner
sensitivity beneath a brash, carefree mask. He tried
to remember the words to a country and western
song he'd once heard that seemed to describe her,
something about a kindhearted woman looking for
a good-loving man. "Do you ever think about going
home?" he asked softly.

They moved forward as the line advanced, and
Stella stared absently at the sequined back of the
heavyset woman in front of her. "Yeah," she admitted, "until I visit my folks. After a couple of
weeks I usually can't wait to get back to Reno. At
least here jobs are plentiful. I'd die of boredom on
the farm."

They chatted desultorily as the line dwindled, and eventually a distracted waitress beckoned them to follow her to a corner table by the window. She provided them with coffee and rushed off to give them time to peruse the menu. While Stella made a visit to the ladies' room to repair her makeup, Joe found himself staring through the window at the casino floor. The glass threw his reflection back at him, and he wasn't surprised at the harshness of the frown that colored his expression.

Joe's conversation with Stella had disturbed him. He was reminded of how drastically people changed, especially if somewhere along the way they made the wrong choices in life. Loving Amber had been the wrong choice for him, but he hadn't thought so at the time. How could he have suspected her to be anything other than the shy, lovely young woman he'd met at an engagement party given for her best friend?

He'd been lost from the moment he first saw her, he thought, closing his eyes with weary cynicism. She had been careful to keep the selfish, pleasure-seeking side of her nature hidden from him. Her outer mask had been demure and caring. Even her background had aided in the deception, he recalled resentfully. Her parents had died in an accident when she was an infant, and she'd been raised by her aunt. The older woman had been a gentle, kind soul who had done more than just accept responsibility for her brother's child. She had loved and protected her charge with a devotion most mothers couldn't equal.

Joe opened his eyes and slowly began to twirl his coffee cup on its saucer. Although she had cared deeply for her Aunt Cecilia, Amber had often expressed regret at her lack of any other relatives. Joe remembered teasing her by insisting she was only marrying him so she could adopt his family. He could still hear the sound of her pealing laughter in his mind. God! He'd been so blindly infatuated, too enraptured with her outer beauty to see her as the calculating creature she'd really been. Joe snorted in disgust. He wondered what Cecilia would think now of the woman her sweet Amber had become.

It didn't bear thinking about, and he found himself unable to reconcile the woman he'd seen tonight with the bright-eyed, laughing girl his heart remembered. Amber had become quiet and withdrawn after her aunt's death, and although he'd worried about the way she'd distanced herself from him he had tried to understand her behavior. He had told himself she was grieving, and that eventually their relationship would once again hold the closeness he'd come to expect.

But it hadn't, he remembered with a vicious thrust of fury, because she'd been too busy comforting herself with another man. Joe clamped his teeth together to suppress a moan, as he remembered returning home from work to find a note propped on his kitchen table. Amber's handwriting had been clear and distinctive, but as he'd read the words the ink had blurred before his eyes.

By the time he'd been able to get his brain to accept the message she'd left for him, his dreams had been smashed beyond repair. He'd been left alone, with only his thoughts of vengeance for company. He ran a tired hand over his grimly set features and once again studied his reflection. He saw a man who was still alone—one whose heart had never stopped demanding retribution.

Three

Joe wasn't aware of Stella's return until he heard the scraping of her chair as she seated herself opposite him. His lashes lifted sluggishly until he could focus on her features, and he realized that her eyes were clouded with more than tiredness when she looked at him. There was concern and understanding in her gaze, and he asked himself why he couldn't feel more than liking for a female who possessed such a compassionate nature. "Because you're still in love with a red-haired witch, Morrow," a taunting inner voice replied. As soon as the thought took form in his mind he thrust it away, unwilling to accept what his subconscious was telling him.

With studied concentration Stella took a sip of her coffee, warming her hands around the cup. Her voice sounded tentative as she said, "Joe, I don't want to butt into your business, but I've been thinking about what you told me. If you still care about Amber Stevenson, it's wrong of me to discourage you."

He grimaced. "I guess I'm pretty transparent."

"So was she, which is why I'm going to help you, Joe. To a gal who's been knocked in the teeth a few times, the signs are unmistakable—and if I'm right, that woman is still very much in love with you."

Joe's heart leaped with an excited throb which he quickly subdued. "Don't let your imagination run away with you, Stella. Amber and I aren't a couple of star-crossed lovers—we're just a man and a woman who never really knew each other."

"Do you want to talk about it?"

Joe didn't attempt evasion, his confused thoughts making him grateful for the opportunity to put an end to pretense. His laughter sounded bleak even to himself as he looked at her. "Don't tell me you can't guess what happened, Stella. I loved her, but that wasn't enough to hold the interest of a woman like Amber."

Stella hesitated briefly, then replaced her cup in its saucer. Leaning forward, she touched the back of his hand. "You still do, Joe."

He jerked back as though he'd been shot, his mouth tightening into a forbidding line as he slumped in his chair. Stella withdrew her hand, her expression contrite as she said, "I'm sorry. I didn't mean to stick my nose in where it doesn't belong."

"It's not that." His dark eyes were shadowed with frustration, and he raked impatient fingers through his hair. "Until I saw her tonight I'd convinced myself I was over her, and realizing I'm not poses a whole new set of problems. Hell, there are so damned many questions I need answered!"

"What do you want to know?" she asked, with a resigned sigh.

"Anything you can tell me."

Stella bit down on her bottom lip, her attention riveted on his closed features. "Even if it's not what you want to hear? I don't want to cause you any more pain, Joe."

"I've been hurting for a long time," he admitted wryly. "A few more blows won't make a damned bit of difference."

"As long as you realize that I'm not positive what's fact and what's fiction. I've only heard a bit of gossip from a few of my friends who work here, but I've known most of them for quite a while and I think they're pretty reliable sources."

"It's enough to be going on with."

At the determination in his voice her manner became gently coaxing. "Are you sure you can take the truth?"

"I'm not sure of my own name at the moment," he admitted ruefully.

"That's what I'm afraid of," she groaned, shifting uneasily. "Amber Stevenson could be more than emotionally dangerous to you, Joe."

His eyes narrowed as he absorbed her nervousness. "Earlier you implied something of the sort. What are you trying to say, Stella?"

"It's just that from the things I've heard, she's been playing out of your league for quite a while."

A cynical quirk at the corner of his mouth lessened the severity of his response. "Let me be the judge of that, and don't make the mistake of underestimating me. Now tell me what you know."

Joe listened to the hiss of Stella's breath as she drew air deeply into her lungs, and he dropped his eyes to his nearly empty cup. Reaching out with both hands, he began to slosh the remaining liquid in a circle. His attention was concentrated on the coffee dregs, his stomach keeping time to the swirling motion. He felt slightly nauseous, no longer so positive that he wanted Stella to answer his questions.

In spite of his denial, he knew she was right to be worried. Amber had almost destroyed him once, and it wouldn't take much for her to succeed this time around. There were so many memories to make him vulnerable, he thought achingly. He saw the naked whiteness of her body twisting passionately beneath his as clearly as if it were permanently imprinted on his mind, and his ears seemed to ring with the sound of her voice crying out his name as he gave her pleasure.

He thought again of that small, condemning piece of notepaper propped up on his kitchen table, and a sudden surge of hatred broke the spell of the past. She'd written, "Forgive me, Joe," as though that one, single appeal could undo the torment of knowing she'd left him for another man. God, he had to be crazy to leave himself open for more of the same!

Yet he did nothing to halt Stella's words when she responded to his earlier demand. "Ms. Stevenson showed up here a few years ago," she explained slowly, "and within six months she'd taken over managing this place. According to my friends, who, I might add, have a good deal of respect for her, the lady is pure steel all the way through."

Stella paused, and Joe quickly lifted his head to look at her. "You're holding out on me," he accused gruffly. "You might as well spill the rest. I'll find out eventually anyway."

Stella began to chew the inside of her cheek, and there was a sheen of tears in her eyes when she continued. "The owner of this casino is a very wealthy and powerful man. From what I've gathered, Amber Stevenson is Theo Carvalho's mistress, Joe."

"I know," he exclaimed in choked tones, a muscle pulsing out of control in his cheek. His hand tightened around his coffee cup until it was in dire threat of shattering. "He's the guy she left me for."

Stella's eyes widened in dismay. "And yet you still want ... ?"

"Wanting is as good a word as any," he snapped defensively. "I don't know how Amber met him, but I need to learn more about Carvalho if I'm going to beat him at his own game."

Stella gasped. "You're crazy if you think you can get her back, Joe. He has her watched constantly. You'll never get away with it."

"You'd be surprised at what I can do if I set my mind to it," he replied hoarsely.

Stella glanced around them, her earlier nervousness increasing until there was real fear in her expression. Leaning forward, she lowered her voice until he could barely hear her. "Knowledge can sometimes be perilous, and fooling around with Carvalho's woman could be deadly."

Joe's features twisted with hatred. "She used to be my woman!"

"Can't you just walk out of here and put her out of your mind?" she pleaded.

"Don't you think I've tried?"

The brevity of his reply was more telling than a fuller explanation would have been. Stella sighed. "He's not a man to tangle with, honey. Theo Carvalho is almost a legend in this town, but not many people can claim a personal acquaintance with him.

His father was one of the most feared gangland leaders on the West Coast in the thirties, and his son grew up with a knack for keeping a low profile."

Joe's lips twisted in a sneer. "That's understandable, but I'm not interested in his childhood, Stella. There's got to be more I can go on. Tell me about the man he is now."

"He's something of a mystery, really. Very few of us would recognize him by sight," she admitted with a shrug, "which means he can move around pretty freely. When he's not working in the office he usually keeps to himself, and only his personal entourage are allowed into his penthouse suite. I've heard that he's almost obsessed with his personal safety, which is something I can readily believe. Although no one seems to know for certain, it's rumored that he still has underworld connections."

Joe lowered his eyes to the table and began to trace the pattern of the tablecloth with his finger. His voice held an ominous quietness as he asked, "Does he have a criminal record?"

Stella seemed perturbed by his apparent calm, and her voice sounded shaken when she admitted, "I don't know. Does it matter?"

Joe smiled coldly and lifted his head until their eyes met. "It might, but that's my worry."

Stella brushed a stray tendril of hair from her cheek, her manner distracted as she interjected a warning. "Someone should worry about you, Joe.

You have the look of a man crazy enough to disregard his safety to get what he wants, and there's one thing I do know. If Theo is anything like his father, he could be a nasty piece of work if he's crossed.''

"So can I, honey," Joe muttered tightly. "So can I."

Amber sat in her office, barely aware of her opulent surroundings. The desk in front of her was of rich grained walnut, the walls a pale gold enhanced by several colorful framed prints, and the deep pile carpeting at her feet was toned in variegated shades of bronze. Behind her the huge picture window framed a sky studded with stars, but she had no interest in the mysterious beauty of the night. There was only one thing on her mind, and it came in a six-foot package of masculine perfection that made her entire body ache with a need she thought she'd forgotten.

For two days she'd been in a constant state of turmoil, because no matter where she went in the casino Joe seemed to appear as if by magic. In fact, magic seemed the only likely solution, since the lower floor of the hotel was immense. It was almost as though he was able to monitor her every move, which was ridiculous. Amber frowned and absently twisted a loose strand of hair at her temple. Other than to nod a greeting he never spoke, and yet she sensed an air of purpose in his manner toward her.

She was becoming paranoid, she told herself, but that didn't stop her fingers from trembling as she remembered the avidity in Joe's dark eyes as he watched her. Usually he was accompanied by his little blond friend, and just thinking of her overblown attractions set Amber's teeth on edge. She could see the obvious closeness between them, and she was shocked by the strength of her own jealousy.

Dear Lord, why hadn't Joe stayed in Los Angeles? What terrible quirk of fate had sent him here, to the one place she'd prayed he would never visit? Hadn't she suffered enough without being forced to come face-to-face with the result of her actions three years ago? The questions skittering through her mind seemed endless, and the answers even more unpalatable.

She felt as if she was being punished for something beyond her control, and she wanted to scream at the unfairness of the destiny that had been charted for her from the moment she was born. With a choked cry she lowered her lashes, and slow, burning tears slid past the dark circles under her eyes. She slumped forward and rested her elbows on the brown felt blotter on top of her desk, covering her face with chilled hands.

"Joe," she whispered in a voice heavy with remorse. "Oh, God . . . Joe!"

Amber felt as though she was dying inside, her entire body shuddering in acknowledgement of Joe's contempt for her. Although she couldn't blame him for his attitude, she had hoped never to have to see that look in his eyes. Her memories of their time together had been so sweet, so unsullied by denial or recrimination. Like an ostrich she had buried her head in the shifting sands of deceit, blinding herself to the chaos she must have left behind her.

Thoughts of Joe had been kept deep inside her where they couldn't be touched, and she had barricaded her mind behind a wall of indifference to cloak the pain. But in an instant those vivid black eyes of his had ripped away her self-protective barrier, and she had been forced to suffer the sins of the past. Now each time their gazes locked, she felt the agony of loss more acutely than she ever had before—and it hurt. Sweet heaven, it hurt so much!

Amber suddenly jumped to her feet, haunted by circumstances that couldn't be changed. She was almost running by the time she reached the door. There were no answers to be found in hiding in here. She desperately needed to be with Joe, if only from a distance. That need was growing with each hour that passed, even though it meant suffering the cutting edge of his derision. If only she could explain—make him understand!

Her hand was on the latch when she halted, slumping against the unyielding wooden panels in defeat. Any explanations she made would mean revealing the secret she'd kept hidden from him. She couldn't afford the weakness of loving Joe, because to do so would mean destroying what pride she had left.

Joe hated her, which was what she had guaranteed when she'd left him. With Theo's help she had achieved what she'd set out to accomplish, and there was no use crying about it now. Straightening, she wiped away her tears with the back of her hand. She had made her choice, and right or wrong she would have to live with it.

It was far too late to wish she could turn back the clock. There was a noble streak in Joe's character that would make it easy for her to take her happiness at his expense, but he was better off without her in his life. She had to continue to believe that . . . she had to! By destroying Joe's love for her, she had freed him to find a woman more worthy of him than she had been. She had sacrificed her dreams to protect his future, and nothing had happened to alter the necessity for subterfuge.

Amber wished she could recapture those months before her Aunt Cecilia had died, if only for a little while. To lie in Joe's arms just one more time, feeling safe and warm, cradled against his strong body. It was the only dream she had left, she realized sadly, but it was an empty one. He was disillusioned and bitter, as he had every right to be. She couldn't call back yesterday and bring to life his love for her. Yet she knew she would rather be with him, even if it meant experiencing his unbridled contempt, than be loved by any other man.

But she had learned to function without futile dreams, and her lips firmed with renewed determination. She had learned to cope with loneliness, and being without Joe had taught her to be self-sufficient. She had undergone an emotional catharsis that had almost cost her her sanity, but had eventually been her salvation. With a strength she hadn't known herself capable of, she had worked to establish her career. Now she was a woman confident of her ability to guide her own destiny. Happiness was unnecessary to survival, she reminded herself bitterly, as she straightened and depressed the handle of the door.

A trip to her private bathroom repaired the damage her tears had caused, and when she stepped into the hallway at least some of her flagging confidence had been restored. All she wanted right now was the comfort of her suite and the solace of the unconsciousness sleep would bring. If she could sleep, she amended wryly, hoping that tonight there would be no nightmares to disturb her rest.

As she walked down the burgundy-carpeted corridor, Amber's usually brisk footsteps were slowed by her saddened state of mind. Since the moment she'd seen him again, Joe had taken over her every thought. Just picturing his face made her shiver, her response to him as strong as it had ever been. He was still the most handsome man she'd ever seen, she decided, swallowing thickly.

His high patrician cheekbones were set in a face of startling beauty, and the slightly olive tint to his complexion portrayed his half-Italian ancestry. She had always loved the long, thick lashes that shaded his piercing midnight eyes, and the slight arch to his brows that made her want to trace them with her fingers. Amber's breath caught in her throat as her stomach cramped with desire.

But she didn't love the changes the years had wrought in him. He wasn't her Joe any longer, she realized sadly. The man she remembered had been smiling, his eyes gentle and tender when he looked at her. Now there were deep grooves beside his mouth and nose and faint lines marring a forehead which used to be smooth. He looked older than his years and forbiddingly unapproachable, with tracings of deep-rooted cynicism overlying his even features.

Joe looked as though he never smiled anymore, unless it was with an edge of sarcasm. But then he no longer had any reason to smile at her. With a swift stab of jealousy she wondered if he behaved differently with other women. Did the blonde he was spending so much time with laugh with him the way Amber had? Did he take her to his room, make love to her? She staggered, her stomach lurching sickeningly. God, would she ever be able to forget the heat of his body against hers? Would the memory of the passionate touch of his mouth and hands against her burning flesh forever mock her?

"Ms. Stevenson?"

The lilting voice calling her name made her jump, and her heart thudded heavily as she turned to greet the woman stepping through the sliding glass door of the office she'd just passed. "Is there a problem, Mary Lynn?"

The flaxen-haired girl offered a pert grin and shook her head. "Not that I know of, but Mr. Carvalho's been paging you. He said if you showed up, you're to meet him at the Oyster Bar."

Amber now had a reason for returning downstairs, and her mouth tightened with annoyance at the sudden leap of her senses. For heaven's sake, she thought in self-disgust, there was no guarantee that she'd see Joe. "But isn't a chance just what you're hoping for, you fool?" a chiding inner voice questioned. "Aren't you hungry enough for the sight of him to turn every opportunity to your advantage?"

She was, although admitting the truth to herself didn't get her anywhere. The fact that their paths seemed to cross so often had to be accidental. Even if she'd like to believe that Joe had inbuilt radar where she was concerned, she knew he wouldn't waste his time searching her out. If anything, he'd avoid her like the plague, and the realization made her flinch.

"I...is everything all right, Ms. Stevenson?" Mary Lynn questioned hesitantly. "You look kind of gray, all of a sudden."

Amber took note of the other woman's concerned expression and attempted a nonchalant smile of reassurance. The result was stilted but apparently satisfied her secretary. "Everything's fine," she said with a confidence she was far from feeling. "I...I'm just a bit preoccupied at the moment. When did Mr. Carvalho leave his message?"

"About twenty minutes ago."

"Thank you."

Amber's poise was somewhat restored by the time Mary Lynn swiveled around to retrace her footsteps, but the closer she got to the employee elevator the more tense she became. If she could only observe Joe from a distance she'd be satisfied, she thought bracingly, not believing for a minute this latest attempt to delude herself. Her fingers were trembling as she reached out to push the down button. "You'll never be satisfied with just a look," that provocative voice in her mind taunted. "You want more than a glimpse of Joseph Morrow...much more!"

As she acknowledged this basic truth to herself, Amber cursed a heart that desperately needed to recapture even a portion of the happiness she'd once known. But Joe no longer wanted anything to do with her, his failure to speak to her these past few days had made that plain. She swallowed past the lump forming in her throat, her breathing constricted. His desire for her was as much a part of the past as the love they'd once shared, and the sooner she accepted that the better off she would be.

Amber walked into the elevator, and the gold-colored doors closing before her seemed somehow symbolic. She existed in a gilded cage of her own making, but the bars that trapped her could never be torn down. She might not be able to forget the dreams of the girl she'd once been, but for Joe's sake she had to remain the woman she'd become. Living a lie was a small price to pay for safeguarding Joe's future. A small...devastating price to pay.

Four

Joe twisted from side to side on the bar stool, restlessness in every taut line of his body. For what seemed to be the hundredth time he glanced at the Rolex strapped to his wrist, cradling a glass in his hands without ever once lifting it to his mouth. While talking desultorily with the bartender, Fred, one of Stella's innumerable friends, he'd nursed the same Scotch over ice for nearly an hour. Now he was uptight enough to drink the damned thing.

Over the past couple of days Stella had introduced him to several people, but only those she trusted to keep their mouths shut. She was worried that Carvalho might find out about Joe's interest in

Amber and do him some harm. She had begged him to wait to see Amber until Carvalho left on the business trip that Mary Lynn, one of the office secretaries, had informed them was scheduled for the beginning of the week. He had agreed, but only because it suited him to do so. Joe wanted to be certain of his moves before he made them, and going off half-cocked wouldn't do much to guarantee a successful venture.

"You've got to be careful," Stella kept reminding him with mulish persistence.

After about the third warning Joe's nerves had been stretched tight enough to snap him in two, and he'd immediately taken his ill humour out on her. "You sound like my father!"

Stella's eyebrows had risen into a surprised arc, her ready smile in evidence as she asked, "Not like your mother?"

Instantly contrite, he'd given her a rakish grin and a wink. "No, Ma would have bashed me over the head by now. Pop's the wily one. He uses his Irish charm to get his own way."

She'd given him a prim, disapproving glance. "Then you shouldn't have any trouble following his example. I've heard about kissing the Blarney stone, but you must have swallowed it whole!"

Although he'd smiled, for his own reasons Joe was determined to be a real chip off of his father's block. He took a sip of the cloudy drink he held and grimaced with distaste. The ice had completely melted, and he hated warm, watered-down Scotch. Plunking his glass onto the wooden bar, he hooked one foot on the lower rung of his stool and shifted uneasily. Where in hell was Stella? he wondered with growing impatience.

She was supposed to meet him here when she got off work and now it was after ten. As usual she was late, he thought wryly, but he had no right to complain. If it hadn't been for her and the freckle-faced Mary Lynn, he would have had no way to track Amber's every move during the last two days.

Joe rubbed his lower lip with a lazy forefinger, and a predatory grin curved his mouth as he remembered Amber's reaction to those apparently casual meetings. Each time she'd seen him she had appeared disturbed and uncomfortable, and the physical awareness they shared had sizzled in the air between them.

When he'd first been introduced to Mary Lynn, he had been surprised at how protective the young girl was of her boss. Her admiration of Amber almost amounted to hero worship, and it had quickly become apparent that she would do nothing to cause the other woman any harm. But then he had remembered how charming and soft-voiced Amber could be, and he'd understood Mary Lynn's quandary. Hadn't he once been taken in by that wide-eyed innocent act himself?

It had taken a great deal of persuading on Stella's part to get Mary Lynn to cooperate, but eventually she'd agreed to furnish them with information regarding Amber's movements. Joe suspected that the girl was intrigued with the idea of playing cupid to a couple of unhappy lovers, as was Stella. The two of them had visions of him carrying Amber off into the sunset, where they would find joy together without the shadow of Theodore Carvalho darkening their lives.

They dismissed the fact that Amber had left him for the other man, either unable or unwilling to ascribe base motives to one of their own kind. Not that he gave them any reason to suspect his motives. He played up to the chivalrous image of a man unable to give up the woman he loved until he sometimes almost believed it himself. Stella and Mary Lynn were romantics at heart, he thought with derision, but he was too damned grateful for their help to spoil their illusions with the truth.

Mary Lynn had provided him with a copy of Amber's busy schedule through the weekend, and when any last minute changes were made she let him know. Tonight she was supposed to phone Stella at the restaurant where she worked the minute Theo Carvalho left for the airport, and once Joe knew the other man was gone he would finally be able to put his plans into action. His tension increased at the thought, and he hastily took a larger swallow of his drink. Considering the number of stakeouts he'd endured during the course of his career, he wasn't handling this waiting game with his usual finesse.

Joe's nerves were raw, his self-control practically nonexistent. Knowing that Amber was so close and yet so far from him was torture in its purest form. The things his inventive mind constantly envisioned for the two of them once they reached the cabin left him in a continual state of semi-arousal, which certainly didn't do much to help him keep a grip on his patience. He had almost forgotten what sleep felt like since he'd found her again, and he'd passed many long nighttime hours pacing across the thick carpeting in his room, his thoughts in too much turmoil to allow him to rest.

But tonight would put an end to the waiting, he reminded himself exultantly. By now Carvalho's private plane should have taken off for Las Vegas, which suited Joe admirably. He wouldn't have to worry about the older man showing up when he visited Amber's suite tonight, and he assumed that she would be more amenable to his suggested tryst, knowing that her lover was out of the way.

Joe quickly finished his drink, yet his mouth remained curiously dry. Fred passed and offered him a refill, but he shook his head in a negative gesture. Right now he needed all his wits about him; so much hinged on this next meeting with Amber. He needed to be calm and persuasive, not drunk and abusive.

With deceptive laziness Joe lifted his hand and stared through his empty glass at the floor show going on above him in the Cabaret Lounge. The distorted image suited his mood admirably. A featureless woman in a gold lamé dress was belting out a jazz tune, while her backup band split and fragmented into an indistinct blur. He only wished he could do the same with his memories of Amber.

Joe found himself wondering about the ways in which Carvalho might have said goodbye to her, and he had to suppress a groan of anguish. His stomach muscles tightened in silent protest. He was revolted by the pictures his imagination was conjuring up, but he couldn't seem to stop visualizing the two of them together. Hell, it was obscene! The bastard must be at least fifty if he was a day.

When he thought about the way Amber was letting herself be used, he wanted to strangle someone. The knowledge that she'd given another man the right to touch her body, especially an aging thug like Carvalho, was eating at his insides like acid. Her reasons for doing so caused even greater bitterness, and he wondered if Amber thought that the financial security she'd gained was worth the price she was paying.

Had she found him easy to forget? After all, it was doubtful if her aged lover was able to provide her with the same degree of sensual satisfaction she had shared with him. When it came right down to the

wire, youth counted for a hell of a lot more than
money where physical stamina was concerned! With
a muttered imprecation he lowered his hand to the
bar and loosened his grip on his glass. His movements were slow and measured, as though some un-
seen force was working at counterpoint to his body.
He grimaced in disgust at the fancifulness of the
thought and rotated his head to relieve the tension in
his neck.

"Sorry I'm late, Joe," a husky contralto apologized breathlessly, "but it was my turn to close the
register tonight."

Stella slipped onto the stool next to him, pausing
to wave at the bartender before curling her hand
around Joe's arm. Leaning toward him, she whispered, "Everything's going according to plan. I
talked to Mary Lynn before I left work, and according to her Carvalho's private plane took off for Vegas at seven o'clock. She promised to call here the
moment Amber leaves her office. It's just lucky for
us that Amber chose Mary Lynn as her personal secretary, or their working hours wouldn't corre-
spond."

Trying not to show his frustration, Joe slanted her
a teasing grin. "You would have made one hell of a
cop, Stel. You really get off on all this cloak-and-
dagger stuff, don't you?"

Stella moved away from him and began to dig
around in her capacious shoulder bag. Her chuckle

was rich and deep as she unwrapped a stick of gum and popped it into her mouth. She gave him an audacious wink as she crinkled the foil in her hand and dropped it into the gold ashtray in front of her. "It breaks the monotony, sugar."

"Where did that sexy drawl come from?" he teased. "In case you've forgotten, you're a Minnesota farm girl, not a Southern belle."

"Yeah, but Mary Lynn's from deep in the heart of Texas." She chewed furiously for a moment, looking satisfied when a series of loud pops issued from between her teeth. "In case you've forgotten, I've been spending a lot of time with her recently."

"Point taken," he said with a laugh.

Just then the red phone attached to the wall behind the bar rang, and both of them jumped. They looked at each other sheepishly as Fred lifted the receiver, waiting until they saw him nod before getting to their feet. "Where is she headed?" Stella asked the balding man as he hung up and sauntered over to their end of the bar.

"Mary Lynn is pretty certain she's making an early night of it," he replied. "The play was pretty light today, and she just finished going over the receipts with the accountants."

"Thanks for your help, Fred," Joe said, holding his hand out to the other man. "I owe you one."

"No sweat," he responded as he shook hands before quickly moving away to wait on another customer.

Turning to Stella, Joe gave her an impulsive hug. "You deserve more than a simple thank you, lady."

To his amazement she blushed, her usual bravado replaced by embarrassment. "You just take care of yourself," she muttered huskily. "I've gotten rather fond of that ugly mug of yours."

Joe had only managed to take a couple of steps when Stella called out to him, and he stifled his impatience as he paused to glance back at her. He was glad he had when she asked, "You won't leave for LA without saying goodbye, will you?"

He shook his head, his expression gentle. "You can count on it."

"Joe?" She gave him a thumbs-up sign and a smile that suddenly held a rather lonely curve. "Good luck!"

As he headed toward the elevators, Joe knew he'd need more than luck if he was going to make it through the days to come. He would need the cunning of a fox, the talent of an actor and a strong stomach to follow through with his plans for Amber. But he would succeed, he thought grimly, because he had no choice. The wheels he would shortly set in motion would inevitably alter his future, and he only prayed he could live with the results.

* * *

As soon as Amber entered her suite she headed directly for the bathroom. For once its sybaritic luxury failed to impress her. The mirrored walls, cream- and gold-veined marble counter and basin and the sunken Jacuzzi, its wide ledge covered with a veritable jungle of potted ferns, seemed unpleasantly decadent in her present mood. Tonight she had found a discrepancy in the books so cleverly disguised that even her accountants had missed it, and she'd had to fire a man who had a wife and three small children to support.

She jerked open the opaque glass door of the stall shower, which was separated from the rest of the amenities by a twisted wrought-iron trellis. As she adjusted the water temperature to her satisfaction, she felt as if she were crumpling under the weight of her unhappy thoughts. She knew she was both respected for her business acumen and feared for her powerful position as Theo Carvalho's mistress, but never more so than an hour ago when Henry Thorpe had entered her office.

The man had looked petrified, his pinched mouth working convulsively as he perched on the edge of the chair she'd offered him. As she began to speak, his face had altered to a sickly gray hue and his eyes had dilated until they seemed to bulge out of his head. When he began repeatedly to run his damp palms over the legs of his slacks, she had known with a stabbing sense of disappointment that there was no question of his guilt.

Until then she had hoped he'd be able to offer some rational explanation, because for years he'd been one of Theo's most trusted employees. It had been Henry who had given her most of her inner-office training, and when Theo had turned the entire management of the casino over to her, it had obviously proved a temptation Henry had been unable to resist.

Amber's mouth tightened, with a combination of anger and pain. The man had underrated her intelligence and abused her trust—but knowing he'd attempted to take advantage of her inexperience hadn't made it any easier to dismiss him. At least the casino wouldn't be pressing criminal charges against him. Theo would probably roar at her like a wounded lion, but she just hadn't had the heart to see Henry's family suffer the indignity of seeing him arrested.

Amber stripped off her favorite dress and wadded it into a ball. Angrily she tossed the vivid turquoise sheath into the open-weave wicker hamper in the corner, with little regard for the future condition of the lovely silk material. Her lacy panties and bra received similar treatment, and she stepped beneath the shower spray with a moan of relief. Quickly she lathered every inch of her body and vigorously shampooed her long hair, the need to feel clean again suddenly paramount.

It took her only a few minutes to towel herself, pat gardenia-scented body powder onto her slightly damp skin and dry her hair. When she was finished she felt more able to face what remained of the evening. Her stomach wasn't in the best condition at the moment, and she decided to forego ordering dinner from room service. She was yawning as she entered her bedroom, and when the doorbell rang she sighed with annoyance.

Grabbing her robe from its padded hanger, she stepped into the enveloping folds and closed it with a yank. When the bell sounded again, she stomped through her living room, her bare feet sinking into the deep pile of the carpet.

These nightly checks of Ray and Bill's were going to have to stop, she vowed, muttering a few choice words under her breath as she applied the safety chain before unlocking the door. Theo's henchmen made her feel about as mature as a four-year-old who needed an adult to check for monsters under the bed before she could trust herself to close her eyes.

When she saw who was standing in the corridor, Amber wasn't entirely convinced that a monster wouldn't be more to her taste. Swallowing convulsively, she stared into Joe's eyes for what seemed an eternity. It took several rapid breaths before she felt strong enough to release the safety chain and stand aside, allowing him to enter her living room. Closing the door, she turned to lean against the wooden panels. As she watched him inspect his surroundings, she was grateful to have a hard surface on which to support her traitorously shaky body.

Joe took in the ambience of Amber's living room with a well-trained eye. It was decorated predominantly in blue and rose, the cream carpeting and walls adding a lighter contrast. Glass-topped tables were placed on either side of a long, classically simple divan in a rose and cream pattern, and a matching chaise longue was angled to the side. The seating arrangement faced a wide expanse of floor-to-ceiling windows, with rose and blue drapes pulled back to expose the view.

It was a comfortable room where a person could relax away the tensions of the day. To the right was a small leatherette-padded bar, and to the left another doorway into what he presumed was a bedroom. Taking a single step forward he caught a glimpse of her bed, and he was suddenly far from relaxed. All he seemed able to think about was how much he would enjoy opening the enveloping robe Amber was wearing, so he could study the contrast of her naked flesh against that dusky rose comforter.

"Wh-why are you here, Joe?" Amber stammered from her position by the door. "Have you come to say...goodbye?"

Joe was pleased by that slight, betraying hesitation in her voice. It seemed to indicate her reluctance to have him disappear from her life, which added a husky pitch to his own voice when he whispered, "No, Amber."

"Why have you come, then?" she asked breathlessly.

Joe's eyes smoldered a heated message across the distance that separated them. "I think you know."

Her hand rose to clasp her throat. "No, I . . ."

"I think you know," he repeated inexorably, his feet making no sound on the deep pile carpet as he moved toward her. "You've known this was inevitable from the moment we met each other again."

Playing for time, Amber straightened and strode past him with jerky movements. Sliding behind the bar, she asked, "Do you want a drink?"

"I want you," he replied, turning to face her.

Ignoring his words, she demanded, "Who told you the number of my suite? It's not common knowledge, and the front desk wouldn't have given it to you without my permission."

"You do take precautions to ensure your privacy," he drawled mockingly, casually seating himself on one of the bar stools. "Tell me, do Ray and Bill give your friend Theo the third degree when he visits you?"

"Of course not, although I can't see what business it is of yours."

"That he visits you?" he asked coldly. "Or that he has to sneak past your bodyguards?"

Amber's only defense was anger, and she tilted her chin haughtily as she said, "Either one. Is that what you did—sneak your way in here?"

"I didn't have to," he said, the smile he gave her not doing anything to soften the febrile glitter in his eyes. "I'm your long lost 'friend,' or don't you remember introducing me to them? Of course the fact that you let Ray and Bill know I'm a cop probably went a long way toward convincing them I'm trustworthy. So you see, my darling, you only have yourself to blame."

"Don't call me that," she muttered indignantly.

Sinuously twisting his body he got to his feet, his gaze locking with hers as he made his way around the bar. "But you are my darling," he whispered with beguiling charm. "You've always been mine."

Amber couldn't seem to move. Her heart was pounding so loudly she feared it was going to leap right out of her chest. Her breath was coming in quick pants as she stared at Joe, the expression on his face unreadable. The hand she pressed to her breast was shaking, and at the touch of her palm her entire body followed suit. Joe was reaching for her when she gasped. "Don't . . . please, Joe," she pleaded.

"You're asking the impossible," he said harshly. "I want you so badly I'm burning up inside, and you want me, too. You do, don't you? Don't you, Amber?''

With a sob Amber turned her back to him and leaned her forehead against the cool roughness of the wall. "What either of us wants doesn't matter, Joe. I have a career and a life-style that's totally opposed to yours. We no longer belong together."

He grasped her shoulders, his grip sure and demanding. "Did we ever belong together?"

"If we did it was a long time ago, and too much has come between us. I'm not the same person I was back then, and there's no way I can change what's happened to me in the interim. I'm a grown woman with a career I take pride in, not a young girl whose only ambition was to be your wife. Even if it were possible, I couldn't go back to being solely dependent on you for my fulfillment, Joe. I enjoy being independent and self-sufficient."

Amber paused before saying with bitter emphasis, "I know what you think, what everyone thinks about me, but Theo has never supported me and he never will. I walk my own path, and I will continue to do so."

Joe carefully brushed her hair aside and lowered his mouth to the nape of her neck. His voice was muffled by the softness of her skin as he murmured, "Do you want to?"

"Do I want to what?" she asked on an indrawn breath.

His mouth slid the collar of her robe aside, and his teeth bit gently into the vulnerable flesh between her neck and shoulder. "Do you want to become my lover again?"

"I can't," she moaned. The heat of his body was pressing against her back, confusing her thoughts until she felt as though she was drowning within the miasma clouding her mind. "It's impossible, Joe."

"Adam lent me the use of his cabin in Coloma," he argued. "We could go there—be alone together for however long we want to be."

"I just can't, Joe."

"Are you afraid of Carvalho finding out?"

It was an excuse she grasped with desperate enthusiasm. "Yes," she agreed quickly. "He wouldn't like not knowing where I am."

Joe gave a harsh laugh. "Don't you mean he won't like you taking another lover?"

Amber stiffened and whirled around to face him. Her head was arched proudly, her voice coolly assured as she said, "No man owns me, but if that's what you want to believe then go right ahead."

Once again his hands cupped her shoulders, this time the pressure barely discernible. Leaning forward until his lips were only inches from her mouth, he smiled at her with seductive encouragement. "You don't have to be frightened, baby. Carvalho isn't expected back from Las Vegas for two weeks, and I promise to be discreet. No one has to know where we've gone or even that you left the casino with me.

I promise to guard that lovely body of yours with as much diligence as Ray or Bill, and with a great deal more enjoyment.''

"How did you know Theo was leaving today?"

The terse question brought his head up in surprise. "Let's just say I have my sources and leave it at that. The only important thing for us to discuss is your willingness to go away with me.''

Amber arched away from him until her back was pressed against the wall, her eyes flashing defiance. "What makes you think I'm willing?''

Before she could stop him his hand reached out and parted the thick fabric of her robe. His eyes devoured the contrast of white flesh against the dark velour. Amber could feel her nipples peaking into tight buds of pure sensation, and the betrayal of her body left her defenseless. Then his mouth began to feast hungrily on hers, and as he cupped her breasts his thumbs brushed sensually against the distended crests.

With mindless compulsion her arms rose to circle his neck, her fingers buried in his thick dark hair. "Joe," she sighed, her breath mingling with his. "Oh, Joe!''

With tantalizing slowness he pulled away from her and closed the front of her robe. "Aren't you willing, baby?''

"Yes," she agreed faintly.

"I've made all the arrangements," he said, careful to keep any triumph from his voice. "Can you get away from here in the morning?''

Now his manner was brisk and completely unloving, and as Amber followed him to the door she looked at him with confused hesitation. "I . . . yes, I can take a few weeks. I haven't had a vacation in three years."

"That's fine," he bit out stiltedly, avoiding her eyes as he threw open the door. "Take a taxi to Harrah's, and I'll . . ."

"Subterfuge won't be necessary," she interrupted him heatedly. "I'm the only one who has any say over my movements."

"Have it your own way, but while you're at it arrange to give Bill and Ray some time off, will you? I don't relish the idea of their following us."

"I will, but . . ."

"I'll meet you in the front of the lobby at two o'clock," he muttered. "Will that suit you?"

"Yes," she whispered.

"Fine, I'll see you then."

Amber watched him stride off and enter the elevator, and as the door slid closed his features were cold and distant. For a long time she stood there, wondering if she had imagined the passion that had erupted between them. She felt the tingling in her breasts and the heated ache of arousal that tensed her muscles in protest. No, she hadn't imagined a thing. Not a single thing!

Five

―――

Amber was wide-eyed with interest as Joe drove his black Chevy Beretta through the rambling, historic town of Coloma. According to what he'd told her earlier, it had originally been part of a Mexican land grant given to a Swiss adventurer who had sailed up the Sacramento River to land at the mouth of the American River. In 1845 Captain John Sutter employed James Marshall, a millwright and wagon maker, and the two men formed a partnership to build a sawmill at Coloma on the south fork of the American River.

When Marshall discovered gold nuggets in the millrace on January 24, 1848, the great California

Gold Rush began. Sadly enough, what meant fortune for others had meant ruin for poor Sutter. Eventually his golden valley was lost to him, buried beneath the feet of countless miners who came for gold and later, with their families, became the pioneers who founded towns such as Coloma.

The sun coming through the window warmed Amber, and she was more relaxed than she had thought she would be. When she had first met Joe in front of the hotel, she'd felt nervous and ill at ease. His greeting had been cool and impersonal, and in growing apprehension she had wanted to escape while he helped the parking attendant load her luggage in the trunk of his car.

Amber had nearly wilted beneath the swift glance of speculation the attendant had given her as he'd held the door open for her to be seated. She had known that leaving town with Joe would cause gossip, but she hadn't realized just how vulnerable it would make her feel. To be fair, the attendant had in no way shown her a lack of respect. Instead he had seemed concerned for her, his brown eyes worried as he wished her a safe journey.

But when the other man accepted the tip Joe placed in his hand, his thoughts had been easy to read. He thought she was using Theo's absence from town as an opportunity to steal some time alone with her lover, and in effect what he was thinking wasn't far off the mark. What he didn't realize, though, was that she had no fear of reprisal from Theo.

Because of his background Theo was a man others regarded with suspicion and fear, the mystery shrouding his past giving just cause for conjecture. For her there was no mystery, only a knowledge that had torn apart her world and reshaped it in ways she hated. She despised the fact that he used others' fear to his advantage. She was certain that he secretly enjoyed the position of power it gave him.

During one of their more heated arguments she had accused Theo of being too selfish to give a damn about anyone else, refusing to believe him when he told her how much he loved her. Instead of responding to the plea in his voice, she had angrily let him know that she didn't approve of the way he hid himself from the world, while he had bitterly admitted how much he disapproved of her refusal to do the same.

If he had his way she would be locked behind doors for the rest of her life, but she had known from the beginning that she could never survive the reclusive, unnatural existence that Theo endured. As it was, her position with the casino and her relationship to its owner set her apart from the people she worked with. They might give her cooperation and pleasant smiles, but they also tiptoed around her, leery of every move she made and every word she spoke. Once she had taken friendship for granted, but no longer. She had almost forgotten what it had been like to share girlish confidences and laughter with someone who could relate to her as an individual.

Perhaps that was why the tension she had experienced when she'd stepped through the revolving doors and first caught sight of Joe had dispersed the instant they drove away from the casino. She had been buoyed up by excitement—a heady sensation of having escaped from a luxurious prison, but a prison nonetheless. As though sensing her need to communicate, if only on a surface level, Joe had casually responded to her questions during the journey and pointed out various areas of interest along the way.

They had been traveling for over two hours when they finally reached the town of Coloma. Joe took a roundabout route, and they passed lovely tree-shaded parks, camping and picnic sights, antique shops, art galleries, quaint restaurants and the John Marshall State Park and museum. It was a beautiful place, and she was pleased when he promised that they would play tourist one day soon.

Once out of town Joe shifted gears and increased his speed, fully confident of his ability to maneuver the vehicle over the twists and turns in the road. Earlier he had pushed a cartridge into the tape deck, and as the tunes played softly she was pleased that he had remembered her favorite type of music. Coun-

try and western songs were well suited to their surroundings, she decided, and with a satisfied sigh she
leaned back against the luxuriously upholstered gray
bucket seat.

"Happy?" Joe asked suddenly.

Amber slanted him a brilliant smile that unfortunately he didn't see, since they were on a two-lane
road and he was preoccupied with passing a lumber-
ing truck up ahead. Surreptitiously she studied his
profile, her eyes seeming to shimmer with warmth as
a shaft of sunlight enlightened their emerald depths.
Joe's bone structure was strong and determined, and
she loved the squareness of his chin. She loved the
widow's peak that pointed toward his broad forehead, his thick wavy hair, the perfect curve of his
ears and the sensual fullness of his bottom lip. In
fact, there wasn't one single inch of Joseph Morrow
that she didn't love, she realized, clasping her fingers tightly together in her lap to keep them from
trembling.

When she failed to respond to his question Joe's
hands tightened around the steering wheel. He hadn't
realized how much he had counted on an affirmative reply, and her silence seemed to imply the opposite. But why should she admit to happiness in his
company, he asked himself bitterly, when he was all
too aware that he lacked the most tangible ingredi-
ent necessary to earn her favor?

Why was he having so much difficulty in accepting her as she really was, instead hungering for the false image he'd once had of her as his ideal woman? His mouth twisted in anger at his own weakness, and this time when he spoke his low tones reflected the vicious derision of his altered mood. "Since we don't measure happiness by the same standards, that had to be the most idiotic question I could have asked you."

"Joe!" His name was a protest as she noticed with dismay the change in his manner toward her. "Of course I'm happy." She glared at him in hurt challenge and added, "Or at least I was."

Giving her a swift appraisal, Joe expelled his breath with hissing impatience. He was furious with himself for failing to hide his resentment from her, which was something he was going to have to be careful of if he wanted his plans to succeed. The idea was to lull her into a false sense of security until she fully surrendered to his seduction, he recalled in disgust, not to frighten her off with his damned temper.

"I'm sorry," he stated heavily. "I guess I'm more uptight than I'd realized. At least now you know how badly I've wanted to be alone with you."

Giving a sigh of relief, Amber nodded her acceptance of his apology. "I understand, Joe. After all this time apart we're almost like strangers, and being together again seems rather unreal."

"Then let's forget the past and learn to know each other as if we'd never met before." After clearing his throat he inclined his head, his manner pompously formal as he stated, "My name is Joe Morrow. What's yours, lovely lady?"

Amber laughed, fully prepared to enjoy the game he was initiating. "My name is Amber Stevenson, and you're the lovely one, Mr. Morrow. I'm only a skinny female with hair as red as a carrot and just as straight."

Joe's mouth quirked into a crooked slant. "You were doing fine, woman," he cautioned with a sidling glance of warning, "so don't blow it. Cute comments like that are strictly forbidden, and you forgot to mention how beautiful you look with those fiery locks of yours down around your waist or draped over your—"

"Thank you, kind sir," she interjected hastily, flushing as she avoided his knowing gaze. She was remembering the way Joe had loved to lie in bed after their hunger for each other had been temporarily satisfied, to spread her hair over his pillow and carefully arrange it across her small rounded breasts.

Trying to ignore the heated response of her body to the memory, Amber quickly turned her attention to the passing scenery. They were following the course of the river, and after Joe turned onto a narrow side road the houses became more scarce and the foliage thicker. Soon the pavement ended, replaced

by gravel. The path they followed was shaded by a
tunnel of tall trees whose branches almost met overhead.

They had been climbing slightly, but after another turn the car began to bump down a dirt road,
where spring rains had carved runnels into the earth.
"Adam and Beth plan on having this section paved,"
he told her. "If you ask me, it'll be none too soon.
The shocks on my car are never going to be the same,
and if it rains we'll probably sink into a bog and
never be seen again."

"Don't be such a pessimist," she reprimanded
tartly, entranced by the rustic log cabin in front of
her. It stood on a slight rise, and late afternoon sunlight glinted off the dusty, paned windows. To Amber, the effect was more welcoming than off-putting.
Although not large, the peak-roofed cabin suited the
beautiful terrain like a wild orchid set in the midst of
a vine-tangled jungle.

Amber drew in a deep breath, and the scents that
wafted through the rolled-down window were sweet
and clean. She could faintly smell the river, and she
turned her head toward the sound of water swirling
and bubbling over rocks. With a muffled gasp of
pleasure she glimpsed the silver, foam-flecked water
a few yards distant from the cabin. Completely enraptured by the perfection of the scene, she cried out
in delight. "Oh, Joe! This place is like a small piece
of Eden, and I love it already."

Joe shut off the engine and glanced at her rapt expression. He wondered how long it would take for her to revert to type and begin complaining of boredom in this so-called Eden. Unfortunately for her, when the metamorphosis came it would make no difference. She was stuck with him here for at least two weeks, and she was going to have to rough it out whether she wanted to or not. Even if she tired of the primitive accommodations, there was no way he was going to take her back to Reno until he had her well and truly out of his system.

Keeping his thoughts to himself, Joe withdrew the key from a magnetic container clipped under the dash. "Come on," he said with deceptive enthusiasm, "let's see how the inside shapes up. The cabin's been empty since December."

They stepped onto a wide, railed wooden porch that wrapped itself around the front of the cabin. As Joe fumbled with the lock, Amber peered over her shoulder toward the trees that lined the river. She saw oak and elm and birch and cedar, and close to the steep riverbank she thought she recognized a patch of feral blackberries. Just the thought of those delicious, sun-warmed morsels made her mouth water and her stomach rumble with hunger.

When Joe's eyebrows lifted in amusement, she blushed and gave a self-conscious laugh. "I'm starved," she admitted wryly.

Joe pushed open the door. "I'll get our things out of the car, and we'll go into town to stock up with supplies and get a meal. Adam tells me there are several good restaurants fairly close by for us to choose from."

"*You'll* go into town to stock up," she corrected firmly, her gaze swiftly encompassing the central living area of the cabin. "There's too much work to be done here before we can be comfortable, and the sooner I've gotten a start the better. If you buy a couple large cans of soup and some French bread, that will do for dinner tonight. Oh, and fresh fruit would be nice," she added absently, mentally organizing her tasks for the next couple of hours.

Joe frowned and bit out tersely, "It's not necessary to make a drudge of yourself, Amber."

She looked at him in surprise, her forehead wrinkling in puzzlement. "I'll enjoy setting the cabin to rights, Joe."

"Then I'll help you, and then we'll go to dinner."

Amber gave a throaty gurgle of laughter and shook her head ruefully. "I don't think I can wait that long to eat."

"Look," he muttered in goaded accents, "there's no reason to act like Little Susie Homemaker with me, honey. I know you're not the sort of woman who enjoys that kind of thing."

Curling her fingers into fists at her sides, Amber carefully wiped her face free of all expression. In a cold, clipped little voice she asked, "Just what 'sort' of woman am I then, Joe?"

Shifting edgily, Joe had to clamp his jaw tightly closed to prevent himself from telling her what he really thought. A muscle pulsed in his cheek, and his eyes became blank and unrevealing as he amended, "Don't get on your high horse. I only meant that you've become used to a glamorous life-style, and you aren't—"

Amber slammed her hands on her hips and interrupted him heatedly. "And I'm not used to hard work, is that what you were going to say?"

His own temper becoming frayed, he glared at her. "If the shoe fits, wear it!"

"After I hit you over the head with it first, Joseph Patrick Morrow," she hissed furiously, her chin pushed forward pugnaciously. "My so-called glamorous life-style exists only in your imagination. I work ten- and twelve-hour days, and believe me, there's nothing glamorous about it. All right, I'll admit that when I'm actually on the casino floor I dress the part, but to me those gowns are nothing but a source of irritation."

Amber gestured downward, drawing Joe's eyes to the tan slacks and the simple, brown and tan button-down blouse she had on. "I much prefer dressing casually, and for your information I take care of my own suite, which completely boggles the minds of the hotel cleaning staff. Like you, they don't think pushing a vacuum cleaner or a mop suits my glamorous image, but I happen to like doing housework!"

Pushing an aggressive finger into his chest, she snapped, "Got it, Mr. Morrow?"

Without warning Amber was lifted against his chest, and her gaze lingered helplessly on the tiny smile that was beginning to curve his mobile mouth. "I've got it, Ms. Stevenson."

"What are you doing?" she squealed in protest, still too emotionally charged to easily relinquish her anger.

"There's at least an inch of dust on this floor and hardwood isn't the most comfortable surface to land on," he drawled softly. "I'd advise you to put your arms around my neck before I drop you."

Amber resisted his demand until he pretended to stumble. With a gasp her fingers clutched at his broad shoulders, before slowly sliding around the back of his head. He was grinning in earnest now, she noticed grudgingly, but she couldn't resist his diabolical charm. With a mock pout that was threatening to turn into a responsive smile, she demanded, "Put me down, you fool."

"First things first," he chided. "Being yelled at by a beautiful shrew has put me in a romantic frame of mind, and this threshold will do as well as any other to carry you over."

Amber's expression softened at his words, but her pleasure at his gesture was lost when she noticed the darkness that suddenly obliterated the amused sparkle in his eyes. Like ink clouding a clear surface, Joe's swiftly changing mood made her feel out of her depth.

Bewildered, Amber looked at his tautly controlled features until sudden understanding ripped through her with the viciousness of a knife thrust. What a fool she was not to have immediately realized how inappropriate being carried over the threshold was where the two of them were concerned. Once the gesture would have meant everything, but now all it did was remind them of a marriage that had never taken place. Amber didn't know whether to laugh or cry when Joe hastily set her on her feet and began to sneeze convulsively.

"I don't think coming here was such a good idea," he grumbled hoarsely, pinching the end of his long, straight nose as he glared at the dusty interior of the cabin in disgust.

Immensely relieved that the tense moment between them had been interrupted in such a mundane manner, Amber couldn't prevent the chuckle that emerged from her mouth. Her voice was gently chiding as she remarked, "Don't tell me you're going to give in at the first hurdle, Morrow? After all, coming here together was your idea."

He held her gaze with deliberate insistence. "Together being the operative word."

Joe's husky voice shivered its message down her spine, and she lowered her head with a shyness that startled her. Her past relationship with this man seemed very far away, as though it had happened to someone else. With a sense of shock she realized that her new awareness of him as a strong, sensual male eclipsed even what she'd felt for him before.

Then she'd been a girl—awkward, inexperienced and frightened of emotions she didn't understand. But now she was a woman, with a woman's needs and desires. The starry-eyed child was a stranger to whom she could no longer relate, because now she was burning inside with the wondrous reality of her own sensuality.

Amber lifted her face to his, and all that she was feeling was there for him to see. "Joe," she whispered.

He closed his eyes, swallowing heavily. As though compelled by a force beyond his comprehension he lowered his head and buried his mouth against the vulnerable arch of Amber's throat. "God," he moaned achingly, "I want you, baby. Tell me you want me, too!"

She shivered at the hunger in his voice, and yet was unable to fully respond to her own desires. The words he had spoken were so similar to those she longed to hear, and yet so very different. Although

they held truth, in themselves they left her feeling
hollow and dissatisfied. For her, the wanting was a
part of her love for Joe, but she knew that the same
no longer applied to him.

When she had accepted his invitation to come here
with him, her eyes had been fully opened to the only
truth that held any reality for her. The reasons Joe
wanted her had nothing to do with loving, she
thought sadly, and everything to do with revenge.
There was too much anger suppressed in him for her
to believe anything else, and although his need to use
her to gain his own ends didn't show him in a particularly good light, she understood the demons that
drove him. Who better? she realized caustically. She
was the one who had given them a foothold on his
heart, so who better to attempt an exorcism than
their creator?

If understanding could be likened to the delicate,
tender budding of a new rose, she thought fanci-
fully, then forgiveness had to be compared to the
beauty of the full-blown flower. In anguished realization she accepted that for Joe, there would be no
blooming. She had dug up the green shoot of his love
with her lies and had buried the remains with her
deceit. Now it was up to her to place a marker over
the grave.

"I want you," she acknowledged quietly. "I want
you, Joe."

But the man who sought her mouth was blind in his willfulness and uncaring of the pain he inflicted. Even as passion flowed like a deep river between them, she felt the savage thrust of his anger. It bruised with its strength and demanded the complete surrender of her will. She gave freely, clinging to him with what little strength remained in her body. With hidden desperation she concentrated on picturing a rose in her mind, and gently began to thread her fingers through the soft hair at the nape of his neck.

That would be her defense when Joe hurt her with the lash of his anger, she decided with an inner strength that surprised her. A rose stood alone and indomitable until it wilted in death, needing only God's tears for succor in a hostile world. So, too, would her love for this man stand alone . . . complete in its own existence. Her breath was a sigh of acceptance, and as her lips softened beneath his he stiffened defensively.

With brutal suddenness Joe tore himself from Amber's arms, filled with mingled resentment and desire. Dear Lord, he thought in confusion, she was already getting to him. Amber felt so right in his arms, so warm and sweet and giving. She was like the sun blotting out the darkness of the past three years, and he was being blinded by its brightness. It was only an illusion, so how could he let her play on his emotions so easily?

All at once he knew he had to get away from her—
to attempt to regain his perspective. Without a word
he turned on his heels and stalked toward the car.
Amber watched him leave with tears flooding her
eyes. As she stared at the uncompromising rigidity of
his back, she tried to gain reassurance by telling herself that sips from his passion now would prepare her
for the years of drought ahead. Years when the rose
would die of thirst until the petals lay withered and
broken and alone.

Six

————

While Joe was gone, Amber washed down the kitchen and relined the inside of the wooden cabinets with an unopened role of contact paper she had found among the cleaning supplies Beth and Adam had left. She had discovered their stash when she had opened the back door of the kitchen and stepped onto a partially enclosed side porch complete with a washer and dryer unit ready for use.

As she worked, her earlier mood of melancholy eased until she was humming a lighthearted tune under her breath. The decision to take one day at a time was an instinctive one, since it was the only solution to the problems she faced. No matter what difficulties arose, she would treasure each hour she could spend with Joe. Like love and hate, it seemed that pain and pleasure were often opposite sides of the same coin. Amber knew she could endure one to have the other. As her Aunt Cecilia had often said, borrowing trouble would get her nowhere fast. In her opinion she had already borrowed enough trouble to last her a lifetime.

After mopping the kitchen floor, Amber felt hot, sticky and in need of a break. While she left the gold-veined linoleum surface to dry, she decided to change into clothing more suitable to a warm June afternoon. Directly off the living room was a short, narrow hallway through which Joe had gone to deposit their luggage before storming off into town. Quickly pushing aside the painful memory, she crossed the hardwood floor with eager curiosity.

Amber glanced into a large, rustic bathroom. A white, claw-footed tub held pride of place along the far wall, and carved wooden cabinets with a heavy marble counter top nearly swallowed the small sink. She had to smile at the charming simplicity of the decor.

Entering the only other room in the cabin, the smile slipped from her face as she nervously observed the wide double bed with its deeply grained walnut headboard. Two identical, single-drawered nightstands bore twin globe-shaped lamps, mock-Victorian in design, which were the only matching items of furniture she could see. Still, with the rounded, log-hewn walls the end result was one of a warmth and coziness that pleased her.

There was a rather battered pine dresser in the corner, and on the opposite side of the room stood a mirrored vanity and chair of a darker wood. When she took a quick look at the interior of the capacious chest, placed beneath a chintz-curtained window, she was relieved to find a variety of folded bedding. Pursing her lips in sudden resolution, she dug through the contents until she found what she needed.

The mattress on the bed was draped with a white sheet, and without further ceremony Amber stripped off the protective covering. There was no way she was going to wait until Joe's return to take on this particular job, since just the thought of such forced intimacy caused the hairs on the back of her neck to lift. With swift, economical movements she three-cornered the sheets, shoved puffy feather pillows into white cases and covered the whole with a heavy down comforter. By the time her chore was completed, she was pink-cheeked with exertion.

"There," she remarked with satisfaction, "now I won't have to see Joe's face watching me from the other side of the bed!"

The sound of her own voice seemed to add emphasis to the visions tumbling helter-skelter through her brain, and she caught her breath at the embarrassing eroticism of her thoughts. She saw her naked body writhing on those cool, crisp sheets while Joe bent over her with insatiable demand in his midnight eyes. They were two halves of a whole, a contrast of dark and light, and as he...

Amber shook her head firmly in an attempt to erase the sensual haze fogging her mind, and decided it prudent to stick to practicalities for the moment. She was already feeling weak in the knees, which caused her some difficulty when she hefted her heavy suitcase onto the bed. She could wait until later to unpack, she decided firmly, withdrawing shorts and a top and laying them on the leaf-patterned comforter.

Grinning with wry self-awareness, she knew that what she needed most right now was a shower—preferably a cold one! Luckily for her, Adam and Beth obviously liked their creature comforts, since the old-fashioned tub had been fitted with a modern overhead shower attachment. After wiping down the dusty porcelain surface, she found towels and washcloths neatly folded on a shelf under the basin. Eagerly discarding her clothing, she quickly stepped beneath the refreshing spray.

The clear plastic shower curtain attached to wooden rungs was spotted with yellow daisies, and as she washed and rinsed her hair she found herself counting them. For a while this kept her brain busy, but when her eyes began to cross she gave it up as a useless enterprise. She was suddenly amused at the lengths she would go to keep from thinking of Joe.

After giving herself an invigorating rubdown with the voluminous gray towel, she dabbed the excess moisture from her hair and returned to the bedroom. Taking a brush from her vanity case, she smoothed out the tangles and tied the long wet mass back to allow it to dry naturally. Then she swiftly changed into a pair of green shorts with a white and green patterned tube top that left her shoulders bare. The stretchy material hugged her braless breasts, following the line of her rib cage and leaving a small expanse of white flesh visible above her shorts.

Feeling cool and refreshed, she returned to the kitchen, her spirits spiraling pleasurably as she observed the effects of her handiwork, her critical gaze approving the shiny counters, clean floor and well-scrubbed sink. Separated from the living area by a high archway, the compact and functional kitchen seemed larger than it was. An old white refrigerator stood next to a black-handled gas stove, both of which she'd earlier been relieved to find clean and ready for use.

Joe had forgotten to turn on the electricity, but enough light poured through the window over the sink to be adequate for her needs. She had thrown open the front door and all the windows when she'd started cleaning, and the slight breeze that feathered across her still-damp skin was extremely welcome.

With renewed energy Amber armed herself with a dust mop and a can of spray cleaner made especially for wooden surfaces, eyeing the living-room floor with resolution.

Turning up the volume on the portable radio she'd dug out of her suitcase, Amber dusted and polished for all she was worth. She rolled up the beautifully designed Navajo carpet which lay in front of the fireplace, admiring the delicate earth tones and the skill that had gone into the weaving. Shifting the heavy brown upholstered couch proved more difficult, and the overstuffed armchairs were real bears.

But it was when she tried to shove the long, heavy dinette table to one side so she could clean under the shag rug it rested on that she had to admit defeat. No matter how she tried, the blasted thing wouldn't budge. Amber considered giving it a good kick with her sneakered foot as she forcefully muttered dire predictions for its continuing existence under her breath.

When a deep voice sounded from the doorway, she let out a startled squeal. "Well, as I live and breathe," Joe drawled mockingly. "If it isn't Daisy Mae come to life."

The hair Amber had tied back at the nape of her neck was defying confinement, and a few recalcitrant strands had managed to escape. With a husky curse that would have shocked her Aunt Cecilia, she tore off the rubber band and threw it at him. Brushing the straggling ends from her fiery cheeks with both hands, she scowled across the room at him. "I didn't hear the car."

Joe grinned at the accusation in her voice, once more confident of his ability to keep Amber at a distance emotionally. During the drive to town and back, he had repeatedly cursed himself for acting like such an idiot. Of course he had reacted to the feel of her in his arms, he'd told himself disparagingly. There had never been any doubt in his mind as to the strength of the sexual attraction between them. Why should he view his physical reaction to her as a threat?

Any healthy, normal male would find his body tuned to a fine pitch when Amber was around, especially when she was dressed as she was now. Joe felt the heat rise in his loins with amused comprehension, his eyes roaming over her scantily clad form with unfeigned appreciation. God, but she was beautiful! The urge to drag her into the bedroom was so strong he immediately began searching for a diversion to control his overactive libido, realizing that this wasn't exactly the most romantic of times to play that kind of game. She looked tired and as out of sorts as a witch with a broken broomstick, and the fulsome pout to her lower lip was thoroughly adorable.

The description was too affectionate to suit him, and he tore his eyes away from her. He glanced at the radio sitting on the ledge above the fireplace. "I'm not surprised you failed to hear me drive up," he yelled over-loudly, his heart thrumming in time to the sensual beat of the music. "It's lucky you haven't caused permanent damage to your ears."

Sticking her tongue out at him, Amber flounced across the room and turned down the volume. "Do you need help unloading the groceries?"

Joe had been leaning against the doorway, but at her grudging offer he shook his head and straightened. "We should give the cupboards a good wipe down first."

"It's already done," she retorted smugly.

With a surprised exclamation Joe swiveled his head to the side and stared at the spanking clean kitchen in amazement. "For heaven's sake, you didn't have to break your back getting all of this done," he exclaimed with guilty disapproval. "Why didn't you wait for me to help you?"

Amber approached him with a militant sparkle in her eyes, ignoring his question as she stared down at the one item of furniture she hadn't been able to move. "You can help me with this monstrosity," she muttered in disgust. "Whoever made this thing needs his head examined."

"How do you know it was a man's doing?"

Amber tossed her head; her hair like a scarlet curtain down her back. "Because it's ugly, and a woman would have better taste."

"Adam would be crushed," Joe remarked, tongue in cheek. "He spent one whole winter on this and those coffee and end tables. He was very satisfied with his efforts."

Joe paused, a malicious gleam in his eyes. "Of course, getting his masterpieces here posed something of a problem. Beth insisted that the money he had to pay for the trailer he hired would have paid for a nice, lightweight table and chairs. She also told me that by the time they had managed to shove this thing through the doorway, she was threatening to offer his woodworking tools to the Salvation Army."

"Smart woman," Amber remarked with heartfelt sincerity. "I think I'd like Beth."

"I'm sure you would," he agreed. "They spent a couple of weeks here during Christmas break, and Adam was indignant when his wife suggested using his artwork for firewood."

Amber began chuckling and gestured to the item under discussion. "If Beth was able to help Adam move his creation from a trailer to the cabin, you and I should be able to shift it a few inches across the floor."

With a devilish light in his eyes, Joe pointed toward the long-handled mop Amber had propped in the corner. "I'll lift the table while you get busy with that thing. Dusting is woman's work."

As he had expected, Amber bristled immediately. "I'll woman's-work you, Joseph Morrow! Now you know why I always insisted that Ma didn't smack you often enough when you were young.''

''I got my fair share,'' he argued, assuming an air of injured innocence that made her want to smack him herself. ''Could I help it if I was a model child?''

Since she had heard innumerable stories of some of the escapades Joe had engineered in his youth, this last bit of prevarication caused Amber to lift her hand to hide an unwilling smile. Shaking her head at him, she said drily, ''You know that's not the truth. According to Ma, after her fifth was born she was just too tired to make the effort.''

Joe acknowledged her hit with a crooked smile, before he once again took note of all the work she had accomplished in his absence. Giving her a rueful grimace, he muttered, ''No wonder Adam wanted me to spend some time up here. This way the worst will be over by the time he and Beth arrive.''

''You always did underestimate your brother,'' Amber agreed teasingly. ''It's always the quiet, good-natured ones you have to look out for.''

Joe's eyes darkened, and his mouth softened with implicit sensuality. ''What about the nasty, ill-tempered ones?''

Amber moistened her lips with the tip of her tongue, her ears attuned to the pounding of her heart. She felt absurdly shy beneath the hooded intensity of that gaze, all too aware of the leashed strength in the body standing so close to her own.

Her awareness was too acute for her to accept it with equanimity, and she hurriedly reached for the dust mop and the can of polish. "All right," she agreed with a shaken laugh. "You lift and I'll dust."

"Coward," he whispered softly.

Amber ignored the sexy rasp of his voice, too discomfited by the leap of her pulse to respond. When he lifted the heavy table, she surreptitiously studied the bulging of his biceps with fascination. He was wearing snug denims and a vivid blue short-sleeved knit shirt. The open collar formed a vee, and the tufts of black hair curling out made her temperature rise to an alarming degree. This time the heat that seemed to be melting her insides had nothing to do with the late afternoon sunlight—and a great deal to do with Joe.

It was six o'clock when they had finally put the rest of the cabin to rights and sat down to the simple dinner of soup and grilled cheese sandwiches she'd prepared. Amber kept her eyes lowered as much as possible, because every time she glanced at Joe the food seemed to stick in her throat. She had the greatest difficulty swallowing at all, and only the cool, sweet honeydew melon that ended the meal proved truly palatable.

"Want to take a walk down by the river?"

"What?" Amber jumped as though she'd been shot, her eyes wide and startled as she stared at him without comprehending a word he'd said.

Joe was well aware of the reason for Amber's air of preoccupation, since he was suffering from the same malady. His skin felt tight and hot, as though the seething cauldron of his emotions was threatening to overflow. He wanted her with a desperation that stretched his self-control to the limits, and every delay seemed to increase his frustration until he suspected he might go crazy if he didn't soon find release.

But it wasn't his mind Joe was concerned with as he got abruptly to his feet and held out his hand to her. The need to touch her took precedence over everything else, his entire body aching for even the briefest of contacts. His chest felt constricted as they strolled down the grassy verge which led to the pebbled banks of the river, and he was all too conscious of the way his body was hardening in anticipation of the night to come.

The warmth of her small hand clinging to his own spread tongues of fire up Joe's arm until he shivered convulsively. Amber must have felt the betraying tremor, because with a muffled gasp she pulled away from him and nearly ran into the sun-dappled wooded area that fronted the wide boulder-strewn river. Her hair was loose and blowing in the wind, the descending sun finding a resting place among the fiery strands.

Joe swallowed with difficulty, and clenched his hands into fists at his sides. He wanted to run to her with the eagerness of a callow youth, but he forced himself to resume his carefully measured tread. Dried bracken crunched under his feet, blending with the musical sound of the swiftly flowing, foam-flecked water. Hidden among leafy branches birds called to each other, their sharp voices similar to that of scolding, twittering old ladies.

By the time he reached Amber's side, the turmoil in Joe's mind had given way to a measure of calm. He knew it was the calm before the storm, but he nevertheless welcomed the hiatus. They walked together for a short distance, until Amber sought the shade of a large, gnarled oak tree. Leaning back against the immense trunk, she surveyed the scene before her with intense concentration.

Joe didn't like the feeling of being shut out—deliberately evicted from her thoughts as though he didn't exist. He wanted her awareness of him to increase to unbearable proportions, until she, too, suffered the agonies of the damned. With a muttered curse he stepped in front of her, the rough bark digging into his palms as he rested his hands on either side of her head.

"Don't run from me," he demanded heavily. "We both know why we're here, Amber."

Amber's eyes were wide and tormented, their emerald brightness dimmed by his shadow, as she studied his grim features. "Do we, Joe?"

Joe hardened himself against her obvious need for reassurance, realizing that the appeal in her trembling voice was a key to unlocking the truth. To turn it would be to expose them to the exigencies of both past and present, and the time was not right for the revelations of his soul. To disclose his motives might weaken him and leave him once again a victim of her feminine wiles. Like a modern day Lorelei, she had the power to lure him to his doom—which was something he couldn't risk.

Deliberately lowering his eyes to her mouth, he whispered, "We want each other."

With a disappointed sigh she closed her eyes and whispered, "Yes, we want each other."

The admission caused Joe's heart to pound against the wall of his chest, and with a groan he leaned his forehead against hers. "It's been so long, so damned long."

In a repetition of countless dreams, Joe watched her slim white hands slide over his chest. When Amber began a tactile exploration, her fingers flexing against the thin fabric, the breath exploded from his lungs in an aroused gasp. Ripping his shirt from the waistband of his jeans, he drew it over his head with barely concealed impatience.

As he dropped it on the ground beside them, he muttered, "Now touch me. Touch me the way you used to, baby."

Amber studied Joe's tense features, and suddenly she wanted to cry for all she had lost. His eyes were closed, his chest rising and falling with the force of his desire. Curling, ebony lashes rested against his flushed cheeks, and she ached to trace their softness with a loving finger. But he didn't want love from her, she realized sadly, because it wouldn't fit his image of the brittle, money-hungry witch he had convinced himself she'd become.

All she could give Joe now was passion, and with a keening cry that expressed a painful need too deep for words she leaned forward to press fevered lips against his hair-roughened chest. She absorbed the scent and taste of his flesh with a hunger she couldn't deny and brushed her head from side to side across the broad musculature of his upper torso.

"Oh, God," he growled urgently. "Are you trying to drive me out of my mind?"

Joe's peaking nipple absorbed the curve of her smile. "And if I am?"

"Then I want more," he said with a shaky laugh, his breath ruffling the hair on top of her head. "For the feel of your mouth on me, I'd gladly spend the rest of my days in a straitjacket."

Tilting her head back, she gave him a provocative look from beneath her lashes. "That wouldn't suit me at all, darling," she murmured with a winsome smile. "Then you wouldn't be able to put your arms around me."

"I aim to please." Eagerly he encircled her narrow waist and pulled her toward the heat of his body with a murmur of pleasure. "Is this what you want?"

What she wanted was for him to love her again, but Amber was a realist. She had learned acceptance in a hard school, and she wouldn't fight against something that couldn't be changed. Linking her arms around his neck, she cried, "Kiss me, Joe."

Joe derived satisfaction from her plea, as well as a need to torment her into further excess. *Tell me you love me,* his mind screamed silently.

When she remained silent, the torment was his. With savage demand he parted her lips, hungrily tasting the inner sweetness she had to offer. The kiss went on and on until he thought the top of his head was going to blow off. With a breathless moan he sought the vulnerable arch of her neck, his mouth passionately pressing against the throbbing pulse that beat at the hollow of her throat.

Joe drew back, his hand tracing the path his mouth had taken. The softness of her skin was a silken temptation to his wandering fingers, and with sensual abandon they moved lower. Then he paused, and lifted the gold heart-shaped locket she wore around her neck. "This is a pretty trinket. I noticed the way it gleamed against your bare skin that first night at the casino, when you wore that sexy black dress with the slit up the thigh."

When Amber stiffened, his head jerked upward in surprise. He noticed the defensiveness of her expression, and his eyes narrowed in suspicion. Returning his gaze to the locket still held between his fingers, he caught sight of a tiny clasp almost hidden by the engraved pattern carved onto the outer edge of the heart. When he pressed it the two sides parted, and he gasped in shock. Inside was the picture of a man, and he sucked in a disbelieving breath. Then his eyes met Amber's, and a cold, terrible anger filled him.

Seven

―――

What in the hell were you hoping to prove?'' Joe's hands were on Amber's shoulders, his fingers digging into her skin when she failed to reply. ''Answer me, damn you!''

''I w-wasn't trying to prove anything,'' she stammered faintly. ''Aunt Cecilia left me the locket, and I always . . . always wear it.''

''With my picture inside?'' he questioned viciously, a disdainful sneer twisting his mouth.

''I . . . yes, with your picture inside.''

''Why don't you just admit you placed it there for effect, hoping I'd see it and come to heel like a well-trained puppy.''

Amber faced him staunchly, but her big eyes were filled with sadness. "Do you think I wanted to precipitate this kind of a scene?"

Joe shook her slightly, his impatience obvious. "Of course not, but I imagine you thought I'd react a little less...violently."

"A little less..." Amber laughed, but the tears that filled her eyes were far from those of mirth. "Oh, yes, you might say that."

Joe's eyes closed briefly, before shooting open to fix her with a steely gaze. "You admit it, then?" he asked heavily.

"What do you want me to do, lie to you?" Amber bit down hard on her lower lip, and gave a rebellious twist of her head. "Well, I won't, do you hear me? Aunt Cecilia told me that the locket was given to her by someone she loved very dearly, and it had great sentimental value for her. It was one of her most treasured possessions, and I wouldn't defile it just to give you a perverse kind of satisfaction. She put it in my hand only hours before she died, and I placed your picture in it. That's the truth, Joe."

"Do you expect me to believe you?"

Although she paled at the cynicism in his voice, Amber proudly raised her head to counter his accusation. "It doesn't matter what you believe."

"Then you won't mind if I go on thinking that this was just a clever little ruse on your part?"

"You're so wrong!" she cried out in frustration.

Joe snapped the locket closed and dropped it as though it burned his fingers. "You're lying through your lovely white teeth, baby."

Amber looked at him pleadingly. "What reason would I have to lie?"

"You tell me!"

"None," she shouted, pushing against his chest in an attempt to escape him. His fingers tightened cruelly, and she gave a gasp of pain. "Let me go, you're hurting me!"

"Not nearly as much as I'd like to," he growled dangerously, his eyes as hard and unyielding as the blackest slate.

With a feeling of sick despair Amber saw that he, too, only spoke the truth. Joe wanted to hurt her, the savagery of his expression left her in no doubt of that. He was a man in danger of losing his self-respect through violence, a man who was being driven to the end of his endurance. This wasn't the sweet, gentle man she had loved, but a stranger who had come to inhabit his body.

Joe heard the barely discernible whimper of his name on her lips, and he shook her again. When she simply looked at him with the clear eyes of innocence he began to doubt, and he hated himself for doing so. She had to be lying, he told himself, but a tiny nerve beside his grim mouth began to twitch uncontrollably.

There was one way for her to convince him she spoke the truth, but he blanched at the thought of asking the one question that was eating him alive. Although he knew he was leaving himself open to more pain, he demanded, "If what you say is true, then why would you want to carry my likeness over your heart, Amber? Why, when you never really loved me?"

Amber opened her mouth to speak, but suddenly Joe couldn't bear to hear her reply. With a groan of frustration his head swooped down and he captured her lips with his. This time what they exchanged couldn't be called a kiss, because there was nothing of tenderness or passion in the merciless taking. It was a furious assault and a mockery of everything a kiss should be, his rage all-consuming, breaking the bonds of rational behavior with exquisite cruelty.

When it was over Amber was limp, her jewel eyes dulled with misery as she looked at him. "Now that you've hurt me again," she whispered with pitiful accuracy, "does the knowledge bring you any real pleasure, Joe?"

"You didn't answer my question," he reminded her, unwilling to accept responsibility for her failure to do so.

With simple dignity, she admitted, "I don't intend to."

"Then let me show you how to please me, my deceitful darling," he murmured in a silken voice that held a threat Amber couldn't ignore.

"Not like this," she gasped when he lifted her into his arms and began striding back toward the cabin. "Please, not like this, Joe!"

"Just like this," he stated coldly. "Over and over again until I've gotten my fill of you."

Amber's fingers were like claws clutching his shoulder, her long hair rippling over his arm as he carried her through the open doorway. As they entered the bedroom she looked at the bed with wild eyes, her struggles only reemphasizing her imprisonment. When he dropped her onto the mattress, her pupils dilated until the black centers nearly obliterated the green.

Tears were pouring down her cheeks as she stared at Joe in horror, flinching visibly as she heard the double thud of his boots hitting the floor. Then he was unbuckling his belt; sliding down the zipper of his jeans. With a strangled cry she struggled into a sitting position, unable to look away from the naked perfection of his body.

"You can't mean to rape me?" she asked, shaking her head in disbelief. "You're not the kind of man who would ever use force against a woman, no matter what the provocation."

"At least you're honest enough to admit that I've been provoked," he taunted, his gaze raking her disheveled clothing in a callous inspection. "But you're not just any woman, Amber. You're ice and fire, and you make my body ache with desire. Take off your clothes for me, baby."

"No!" she shouted.

"Why not, you're nearly naked already. Wasn't that part of the game?"

"There was no game," she almost sobbed.

"Then what was that touching little scene with the locket meant to prove?" he snapped angrily. "Wasn't it just a prop to bring me to my knees?"

Amber's head drooped like a wilted flower, her eyes closing in despair. "I could never bring you to your knees, Joe."

A reckless laugh rang out, making her cringe. "There was a time I would have crawled to hell and back for you, but you know that, don't you? You enjoyed the power it gave you, Amber. That kind of supremacy over another human being is like a drug, and it's obvious to me that you're craving another fix. It's the kind of turn-on you wouldn't have with your current lover, because he's past the age to be taken in by a mercenary little tramp like you."

Amber's body jerked as though a whip were flaying her tender flesh, her hand lifting to ward off the viciousness of his words. "Oh, God," she sighed in defeat. "What can I say to convince you how wrong you are?"

With total unself-consciousness he moved toward the edge of the bed. "You don't have to say a thing, Amber. We don't need words between us."

Suddenly she straightened, her body stiffening with pride. "I just have to lie here and let you use me, is that the idea?"

Joe drew a taunting finger across the delicate line of her jaw. "We'll be using each other."

Amber drew in a deep breath, her eyes flashing defiance as she jerked away from his touch. "And if I refuse to comply, what then? Will you go ahead and rape me, Joe?"

His mouth compressed into a hard, unyielding line and he grabbed her face in his hands. Forced to meet his smoldering gaze, she repeated, "Will you, Joe?"

"It won't be rape," he gritted through clenched teeth.

"Then what would you call it?"

Joe's fingers began to probe the trembling corners of her mouth, brushing away the tears from her cheeks as he did so. "This time we'll meet as equals, Amber. I'm no longer the besotted idiot ready to worship at the shrine of your womanhood, and now you have no reason to pretend to be something you're not."

"You don't know the first thing about me," she cried bitterly. "You're too blinded by your need to get even with me to see anything clearly."

Joe was shaken by her perception, the color draining from his face as he stared at her. "How long have you known my intentions?"

"From the beginning," she admitted tiredly. "There was hate and a need for revenge in your eyes when you looked at me and in your voice when you spoke. After that first night you appeared indifferent, but I could feel you staring at me everywhere I went. You seemed to know where I was going to be before I did myself, and our meetings occurred too often to be mere coincidence. Were you having me followed, Joe?"

"A friend kept me informed of your schedule."

"Your little blond bombshell?" she questioned jealously.

Joe's mouth twisted into a smile of derision. "Let's just say that she aided and abetted me and leave it at that."

Amber couldn't stop herself from showing her resentment of the other woman, the jealousy still in her voice when she asked, "Is . . . is she your lover?"

"No, but she is a good friend," he remarked bluntly. "I want her kept out of this, Amber. She's too nice a woman to suffer because she cared enough to help me."

Amber shook herself free of his confining hands, a look of pained bewilderment in her eyes. "You know I'd never purposely hurt anyone!"

"Carvalho might," he stated coldly. "When he finds out about us I don't want him taking his anger out on Stella."

"That's h-her name?"

"Yes, but I want you to forget it," he muttered warningly. "She's innocent of any wrongdoing, and I won't have that bastard giving her trouble."

"He's not some kind of monster, Joe."

His dark brows formed a skeptical arc. "From what I've been told he's descended from one."

Amber bit her lip and avoided his gaze. "Theo can't be held responsible for the things his father did."

Angered at her defense of the man he hated, Joe's voice held bitter condemnation when he snapped, "It's in the blood, and Carvalho's is tainted with the sins of his father."

She whitened, her features suddenly appearing pinched and ravaged. "As you say," she remarked tonelessly, "it's tainted blood."

Tired of the direction their conversation had taken, Joe asked the question most on his mind. "If you knew this wasn't to be a lovers' reunion, then why did you come away with me?"

Amber shrugged dismissively, a defenseless droop to her smooth shoulders. "I guess because we're two of a kind, Joe. We stumble about in the darkness of our hearts, groping at anything that might seem real and hitting out at anyone who tries to help us."

"If that were true I wouldn't be here with you now, because the last thing you are is real. You're a figment of my imagination, but you won't be for long."

Joe placed one knee beside her on the bed. His dark skin gleamed like oiled teak in the fading light filtering through the window, and Amber felt faint with irrepressible longing. She wanted to run her hands over the honey-gold surface of his warm flesh and press her lips to the pulse throbbing against his brown throat. He had all the male power of a pagan god as he arched toward her, and she began to shiver uncontrollably as he slowly smoothed his palms over her bare shoulders.

Unable to hide her response to his touch, she slid a nervous tongue tip across her slightly swollen bottom lip, and gazed at him with apprehension. "What do you mean?"

"The blind learn to see by touch," he replied huskily. "By the time we leave here we'll both have what we've needed from each other, Amber. You've hinted often enough that you want me to see you as you really are, and in doing so I'll finally be able to rid myself of the specter of the woman I thought you were. Tit for tat, darling," he drawled sardonically. "A fair exchange, wouldn't you say?"

She shook her head, bracing her hands behind her and leaning as far away from him as she could get. "Your thinking is a diabolical pattern for destruction," she gasped. "It would be like making a pact with the devil. Can't you see that, Joe?"

The expression in his eyes held all the wicked charm and sorcery of that dark angel, thrust from heaven by an angry God. "You cast out the light and plunged me into hell with your lies, Amber. Don't you think it poetic justice that you be the one to share my fate?"

Amber closed her eyes tightly to block out the sight of that beautiful face, haunted by the bitter shadows of the past. When he pushed her back on the bed she felt numb, and when he removed her clothing she pictured her lovely, perfect rose in her mind. It was a protective talisman, shutting out the pain and reminding her of her responsibility to this man she had inadvertently hurt so cruelly. She had come here to try to heal the bitterness between them, and she would stay in an attempt to give him back the pride and dignity he had lost because of her.

Amber felt Joe's hands begin to trace the curves of her body as he sat beside her, and the feelings that surfaced in her at that moment melted the ice that had encased her heart for so many years. His touch was gentle and almost reverent, and she could feel his fingers tremble against her skin. There was nothing of anger or punishment in his tender exploration, and her sighs blended with the harsh acceleration of his breath.

It was then that hope blossomed like the rose, and she knew that finally she could free herself from the guilt of the past. She could make amends for all the pain she had caused him. Her own pain she could bear, because it was something she'd learned to live with over the years. Although she had repressed her love for Joe, it hadn't died and never would; she didn't want it to. Now she would use the strength that knowledge gave her to heal his wounds and set him free of the twilight world he inhabited, regardless of any new scars she herself would gain in the process.

With exquisite hesitation Amber's arms stole around Joe's neck, her lashes lifting to observe the momentary shock and confusion in his eyes. A small, secretive smile curved her lips, and with a groan he sought her temptingly pouting mouth with the desperation of a starving man. There was no longer any need for words between them, their desire for each other needed no verbal confirmation.

Their loving was wild and uninhibited, their concentration on each other total. In that final moment of possession Amber screamed in ecstasy, tears flooding her eyes as she became whole again in her lover's arms. If there was a brief expression of triumph on Joe's face, it rapidly disappeared beneath the peaking tide of his own pleasure. Soon it was he who was shuddering weakly against her moist flesh, captured by the silken sheath of her body. As the tears dried on Amber's cheeks, it was Joe's groaning cries she heard as she languidly drifted into sleep.

Joe stood on the porch watching the dawn of a new day. He cradled a mug of coffee in his hand, a pair of ragged denim cutoffs his only adornment. As he ran the fingers of his free hand through his shower-dampened hair he arched his back. Feeling the pleasurable stiffness in his body, Joe smiled. Amber was everything he remembered and more, he mused thoughtfully. Their lovemaking had always been special, but her maturity had added a new, spectacular depth to the explosions of rapture they'd experienced last night.

They hadn't done much resting, that was for sure. Now Joe had decided to let her sleep, dragging himself from the bathroom into the kitchen so he wouldn't be tempted to reach for her again. God, he decided with an unexpected surge of self-disgust, he'd behaved like a rutting stag. Each time he'd drawn her against his hotly aroused body Amber had been totally responsive to his demands, but that didn't make him feel a damn bit better. He was appalled by the extent of his need for her and suddenly angry with her as well as himself.

Joe realized that he'd been right to compare Amber's power over him to some kind of erotic drug, but last night had proved to him that he had been the one in need of a fix. How could he hope to keep his emotions unfettered, he asked himself savagely, when she gave herself to him with all the warmth and sweetness he'd known in the past?

That passionate giving was the reason for his present turmoil, because he realized there was no longer any pretense between them. Because of a picture in a stupid little locket he'd thrown away any advantage he might have had with her, and now he was going to have to pay the price. According to Amber, she'd guessed his true motives for bringing her here from the beginning. Considering her intelligence and her past knowledge of him, he should have considered that possibility.

But he hadn't, he thought cynically, and now all his careful scheming was shot to hell. Amber was certainly too smart to whisper love words to a man bent on revenge, and he was sick to death of the situation he'd created. Add to that his physical and emotional vulnerability, and he knew he'd been caught in his own trap. After last night any remaining scales had been ripped from his eyes. To spend more time alone with her would be madness.

Joe took a deep swallow from the mug he held and watched the river flow past in the distance. The water splashed and gurgled over the rocky riverbed, while overhead the sun enhanced the spray with sparkling prisms of light. Amber had called this spot an Eden, but for him it was a place of shadows. He was caught somewhere between light and darkness, and his mind was screaming at him to escape before it was too late.

When soft arms stole around him from behind he stiffened defensively, and drew an unsteady breath into his lungs. "Good morning," he muttered harshly. "Did you sleep well?"

"Mmm, but I didn't like waking up alone." Her laughing voice rippled over his sensitized nerves, instantly causing the blood to flow through his veins in a molten flood tide of incredible force.

Dislodging her arms from his waist, Joe turned to face her and nearly stopped breathing. Amber's long hair was like captured sunlight, stark and pure against the white cotton blouse she wore. Blue corduroys enhanced her long legs, but after a cursory inspection his attention returned to her face. Those lovely thick-lashed eyes of hers stared at him with emerald fire in their depths, and her skin had the translucent quality of the most exquisite pearl.

"Joe, are you all right?" she asked suddenly, laughter still shading her voice. "You're looking at me rather oddly."

Jolted from his preoccupation, his low tones were brusque and hostile. "You're imagining things!"

Immediately the smile slipped from her rosy lips, and she moved to stand next to him. She was staring fixedly toward the river when she said, "It's a beautiful morning. What do you have planned for today?"

The question was an innocent one, and yet it fired Joe's antipathy. Anger was an emotion he could understand, one he'd experienced often enough when thoughts of Amber had returned to haunt him. This was what he'd expected from her, he told himself, only it had come sooner than he'd planned. Paradoxically, he didn't stop to question the reason for the relief he was feeling.

Instead he reminded himself that Amber was fashioned for silks and bright lights, not homespun and candy floss. She wanted more than the clear, sparkling brightness of sunlight for adornment, and she wanted more than him to make her life satisfactory. All he was good for was playing the stud, and that just wasn't enough for him.

Abruptly he angled his head toward her, his voice scathing. "Do I have to make plans for your entertainment?"

Amber's chest rose with the force of a swiftly indrawn breath, yet her low tones held only the merest tremor when she replied, "No, I'll enjoy being lazy."

Joe snorted with sarcasm and quickly finished the rest of his coffee. "Do you need to rebuild your strength after one night with me, honey? Obviously your precious Theo isn't keeping you in shape."

"That was crude and uncalled for, Joe."

He shrugged his shoulders, and gazed down into his empty mug. "I'm a crude man, or haven't you figured that out yet?"

Amber turned toward him and placed her hand on his hair-roughened arm. "You never used to be," she whispered. "You were always thoughtful and kind and considerate of my feelings."

"That was a long time ago," he retorted with a heavy sigh. "I'm not the man you knew, and you sure as hell aren't the woman I remember."

"I thought..." She paused, her voice faltering as she met the hard glitter of his eyes. "I thought by being here together we'd learn to respect the people we are now, Joe. Couldn't we at least try, if for no other reason than to put an end to all the hating?"

Instead of answering her question, he blurted, "I think it's time we returned to Reno."

As soon as the words were out of his mouth Joe wanted to call them back, especially when he saw Amber's stricken expression. But his own personal demons were riding him, and just the fact that he found the thought of leaving here painful was enough to determine his course.

"Why?" She steadied her bottom lip with her teeth, her eyes wide and tormented as she looked at him.

"Because I'm tired of playing games, and there's no longer any reason to stay."

"You got what you wanted from me last night," she remarked hollowly.

Joe looked at Amber, and suddenly he knew he couldn't go through with it. They would be forced out of their Eden eventually, but while they were here he would take whatever she was willing to give him. Already the thought of being without her was tearing him apart, and the knowledge neutralized any need for revenge. Finally he could accept that no matter what happened in the future, a part of him would always belong to this woman. That's why he had never become reconciled to losing her—why he'd shielded himself from the truth with hatred. For better or worse her pain was his pain, her regrets were his regrets, and—God help him—her heart was his heart.

With a strangled cry he pulled her into his arms, barely noticing the sound when his coffee mug shattered against the wooden porch. "No," he groaned hoarsely, burying his mouth against her beautiful hair. "I'll never get enough of you, baby. Never... never..."

His admission tore away Amber's remaining restraint, and she couldn't hold back the admission she'd been longing to make for so long. Nearly choking on sobs, she cried, "I'm not Theo's mistress, Joe. I swear I'm not and never have been. Please...please believe me. You're the only man I'll ever want."

Joe looked at the earnest little face turned up to his, and he began to shake with a relief so great that he wanted to get down on his knees and give thanks. She was his, had always been his, and he sighed his answer against her trembling mouth. "I believe you, honey."

Joe rained kisses over her flushed cheeks and teary eyes, lifting her into his arms and carrying her back inside. Amber's lips stopped trembling as she clung to him, her body pliant and yearning. "I love you," she moaned against the warm curve of his neck. "I love you, Joe."

Gently he laid her upon the rumpled bed and pleaded, "Tell me again, Amber."

"I love you," she repeated, "I'll always love you, Joe."

Instead of triumph, Joe felt humbled by her admission. He had wanted revenge and had been given back his reason for living. He had sought restitution for all the pain of the past and instead had found new hope for the future. He had wanted to hurt her. Instead she'd healed his wounds.

"I love you, too, baby," he whispered. "I love you, too."

Eight

Amber wound the reel she held, her expression one of intense concentration. She was eager to land the fish struggling on the end of her line, especially since Joe hadn't caught even one that morning. But the fish was equally determined not to become dinner, and she hadn't expected such stubborn resistance. "Net it, Joe," she squealed nervously.

"I thought you wanted to do this all by yourself?"

She slanted him an irritated look. "I've changed my mind."

With a shout of laughter he shook his head, eyeing her exertion with complacency. "No can do, sweetheart."

For several minutes that seemed more like hours to Amber, woman and fish battled valiantly. But then Amber, goaded by the critical taunts of the man propped up on his elbows beside her, gave a mighty yank of the rod. Her fish flew into the air and slapped the smug grin off Joe's face. Sputtering, he jerked himself into a sitting position and glared down at the wet creature now flopping in his lap.

"You did that on purpose," he accused indignantly.

Amber laughed until she was doubled over, tears of mirth flooding her eyes as she grabbed at her stomach. "Oh, Joe," she gasped between giggles, "if only you could have seen yourself when that fish smacked you. You looked so...so funny!"

"I can imagine," he drawled, his eyes never leaving hers as he started to get to his feet.

Stepping off the edge of the blanket that contained their picnic lunch, Amber backed away from him. "Now, Joe," she choked breathlessly, "don't do anything hasty."

Joe gave her a look of innocent incomprehension as he pulled the hook from the fish's gaping mouth. Dropping the pliers back into Adam's battered tackle box, he asked with exaggerated mockery, "Why are you so nervous all of a sudden, Amber?"

One of the sun-bleached pebbles that lined the shore had found its way inside her brown leather sandal, but Amber didn't pause to dislodge it. She didn't trust that gleam in Joe's eyes one little bit, and she wasn't too fond of the way he was clutching that poor dead fish, either. Giving him a pacifying smile, she continued to back away from his steadily advancing figure.

"Why don't y-you put my fish in the ice chest so w-we can wash up for lunch?" she stammered, wincing as the stone dug into the arch of her foot. "We've been out here since sunup, and I—I'm starved."

"I want to try a little experiment first," he responded with a grim smile, stalking her like the big, confident male animal he was. "I read somewhere that fish oil is good for the complexion, and we should do our best to keep you looking beautiful."

"You wouldn't dare," she gasped, eyeing the dead fish with loathing.

"Damned right I would," he retorted cheerfully.

"I...it was an accident," she protested, quickening her retreat. "I didn't deliberately shove that thing in your face."

"No, but I'm going to shove it in yours," he stated with undisguised relish, closing the distance between them with determined strides. "I'll teach you to laugh at me, woman!"

Amber's voice was caught between laughter and a shriek as she turned to run, sprinting up the bank without being slowed down by the pebble one jot. She had just reached the grove of shady trees when she made a very serious tactical error. Glancing over her shoulder to check Joe's position, she tripped on a tuft of long grass and went sailing.

Before she could catch the breath that whooshed out of her lungs when she landed on the hard ground, Amber was being rolled onto her back. No sluggard when it came to seizing an advantage, Joe straddled her body. Clamping her wriggling hips with his muscular thighs, he grinned down at her devilishly. Holding the fish in his right hand, he pressed his left against her chest to keep her prone.

"Take your punishment like a man," he demanded.

"I'm not a man, and don't wave that thing under my nose."

Bits of dried bracken and weed were caught in her hair, the gloriously tangled mass framing her small, indignant features in a reddish-gold nimbus. Joe's gaze traveled to the flesh exposed by the vee of her simply tailored sleeveless blouse, approving of the light tan she'd acquired during the past two and a half weeks. As his inspection continued downward, past violently heaving breasts to where his lower limbs cradled her bucking hips, his mouth formed a sensual curve of appreciation.

"Believe me, baby, your sex is in no doubt," he uttered softly, tossing the fish away with a careless flick of his wrist.

Amber saw it land and quickly averted her head from its glassy eyes. It seemed to be staring at her accusingly, and she felt an insane urge to tender an apology. Giggling again, she exclaimed piously, "Thank God, Joe! You had me worried there for a minute."

"Did I?" he mused with thoughtful preoccupation, his eyes apparently permanently glued to her waist and hips.

Flushing under the intensity of his masculine appraisal, she questioned him with increasing embarrassment. "Why are you staring at me like that?"

"I was just thinking how much better you look in jeans than I do."

Amber gave him a wary glance of suspicion before acknowledging the compliment. "Thank you."

Joe nodded courteously, but there was a distinctly predatory gleam in his dark eyes as he inspected the snap at her waist. "I really should find out why."

By the time Amber realized his intention it was too late. His busy hands had dealt with her zipper and the snap on her jeans, and his fingers were fluttering against the lower left side of her stomach like trapped moths. The feeling was a refined form of torture, and she found herself pleading for mercy before many minutes had passed.

Laughing uncontrollably, she gasped. "No, don't...oh, I've got a stitch in my side."

"Ahhh," he chortled with a pleased smirk. "I thought I'd find your ticklish spot if I searched long enough."

"You knew very well where it was," she cried as his fingers wriggled with increasing fervency against her sensitive flesh. "Stop...please! I can't stand it!" she managed to say through her laughter.

"What will you give me if I do?"

Tears of mirth blurring her vision, she frantically sought a peace offering. "I...I'll fry my fish for your dinner."

Joe shook his head. "Not good enough, honey. Since it was my face that was attacked, I've already claimed that fish as a prisoner of war."

Since he was the obvious victor of this particular engagement, she knew the deck was stacked against her. Giving him her most winsome smile, she tempted him without an instant of remorse. "I'll fix my special potato salad to go with it."

Joe's hands shifted to cup her cheeks. "Promise?"

Amber should have just given her word and escaped, but some imp of mischief made her wrinkle her nose and remark disapprovingly, "You smell like fish."

"No, you do!"

His shout was a male paean of triumph, and then he was vigorously rubbing his palms all over her face. Like two children he and Amber were soon rolling around on the ground, laughing boisterously as they pummeled and prodded each other. But suddenly both were still, their rapid breathing altering subtly as an extremely adult awareness ended their game.

"Now we both smell fishy," Joe murmured huskily. "Why don't we go take a shower?"

Amber's eyes had darkened in color, the tumult of her emotions lending them the mysterious shadings of a primeval forest. Wrapping her arms around his neck, she gave him a provocative look from beneath sooty lashes. "We left our lunch by the river," she reminded him with a teasing smile. "Aren't you hungry?"

The tip of Joe's tongue probed the corner of her moistly tempting mouth, as he whispered, "Are you?"

"Only for you." She sighed. "Only for you, Joe."

Amber sat alone beneath the spreading branches of the oak tree, her gaze pensive as she stared into the gathering darkness. Joe had gone into town to fill the car with gas, since there was a chance that they wouldn't be able to find a station open in the morning. They were leaving early, the Beretta's trunk already filled with their suitcases. He hadn't asked her to go with him, but then she hadn't expected him to.

The past few days had been crammed with activity. Joe was no longer satisfied with the environs of the cabin and they had explored Coloma and the surrounding countryside until they were both too exhausted to do more than shower and crawl into bed at night. Joe's moods had fluctuated from dour taciturnity to an almost wild gaiety, but Amber had understood. Neither of them wanted to face the fact that their time together was coming to an end.

A hard knot seemed to have permanently lodged itself in her throat, and she swallowed past the constriction with difficulty. Her eyes were dry and burning, the result of the tears she'd shed as she watched Joe's car disappear down the road. It had seemed so symbolic at the time, him driving away while she was left behind. She had cried until she was drained and empty—and more alone within herself than she could ever have imagined being.

But it was a feeling she was going to have to get used to, she told herself staunchly. By this time tomorrow they would be back in Reno, and soon after that Joe would leave for home. They would go on with their lives separately, and soon these days they'd spent together would seem like a vague, beautiful dream. Amber pressed her lips tightly together, the corners holding a downward droop that conveyed her emotions better than words. Oh, God, she didn't think she could bear it!

Slowly getting to her feet, she retraced her steps to the cabin. Upon entering she looked around, trying to memorize every beloved nook and cranny. She glanced toward the lumpy couch where she and Joe sat most evenings, the cool night air giving them an excuse to use the cavernous rock fireplace. They would snuggle there in the darkened room, her head on his shoulder as they stared at the dancing flames and talked.

As the halcyon days passed they had drawn closer together in spirit, and Joe had gradually lost all traces of his earlier defensiveness with her. He had discussed his family, his work as an undercover agent and, on one particular evening, he'd mentioned his recent promotion to detective status.

"I turned it down, which is why I was advised to take some time off," he admitted with a wry twist of his lips.

She stared at him in bewilderment. "But why, Joe? It's what you always wanted."

Joe evaded her eyes. "I've gotten used to working the streets, Amber."

"You mean you need the thrill of putting your life on the line," she amended bitterly. "I did that to you, didn't I? Taking that kind of risk was your way of getting back at me for leaving you."

Joe brushed his mouth against her temple, his arm drawing her closer. "In the beginning maybe I was just trying to forget. But eventually the work I was doing became a satisfaction in itself. I don't know if I can do without it now, Amber. Do you understand?''

''But you never volunteered for that kind of detail when we were together, Joe.''

''I had different priorities then, honey.''

Yes, she had wanted to tell him. *You wanted a home and children, but I destroyed those dreams for you.*

God! How badly she had wanted to plead with him to give up his undercover work and take that promotion. But she had remained silent, knowing she had no business trying to influence his future. She had given up that right when she left him, and she'd known that no matter how much she wished differently she had nothing to offer him as an inducement.

With a muffled cry Amber turned to stare out of the window, but the rapidly darkening view didn't ease her inner torment. Her gaze was drawn to the copse of trees by the river. It was on another twilight evening such as this that she and Joe had lain side by side, waiting for the stars to appear overhead. They had been holding hands, and she had been peacefully contented.

Joe had turned his head toward her and asked gently, ''What are you thinking?''

She smiled and traced his mouth with her forefinger. ''That I've never been so happy.''

A shadow of pain convulsed his features, and he had quickly averted his head. After a moment's tense hesitation, he asked, "Amber, were you happy with me...before?"

There was such a depth of vulnerability in his voice that she cried out and threw herself against his chest. "You know I was," she gulped tearfully.

Joe wrapped his arms around her so tightly she could hardly breathe. "Then why did you go away?" he cried tormentedly.

"I can't explain," she whispered, "but it wasn't because I stopped loving you, Joe."

He shifted restlessly, lifting her head with a gentle hand beneath her chin. "I know you enjoy your work at the casino, but you're not a hard-boiled career woman, Amber. You were fashioned for love and a home and children, and I think deep in your heart you know that's true. I believed you when you told me you'd never been Carvalho's lover and I no longer think you were drawn by his wealth. God, you're like a puzzle with pieces that just don't fit, and it's driving me crazy! What kind of hold does he have over you, baby? Don't you know you can trust me to help you if you're in some kind of trouble?"

"I'm in no trouble," she replied stiltedly, "and you're wrong, Joe. Thanks to Theo I have a career I enjoy very much. I like being independent and productive, and I don't want to be tied down to a house and babies. That was your dream, Joe...not mine."

The enormity of the lie she'd just told him caused her to shiver, the blood seeming to freeze in her veins. She squeezed her eyes tightly shut but wasn't able to prevent the hot tears from scalding her cheeks. "Please, I don't want to talk about it anymore."

Joe's voice grew cold and distant. "Then there's no point in asking you to come back with me?"

"None." She sighed dejectedly.

When he rose to his feet, her arms had ached to hold on to him and never let go. His body had been stiff with rejection as he moved away from her, pride in every rigid muscle of his back. But he had looked so lonely as he stood by the riverbank, she remembered, his tall figure bathed in moonlight. So lonely and hurt and defiant, and there had been nothing she could do to ease the blow she'd just inflicted on him.

With a sigh Amber moved away from the window and wandered listlessly into the bathroom. Even here memories tormented her—of Joe shaving while she sat on the edge of the bath and teased him about the faces he was pulling, of the two of them playing in the shower until passion overcame their need to be clean, of their hands languidly exploring each other while they lay immersed up to their necks in bubbles. So many precious memories. Enough to last her a lifetime?

No! At the thought Amber's head lifted, a sparkle of determination in her eyes. They had one last night together and she was damned if she was going to waste it feeling sorry for herself. Tonight belonged to Joe, a last tribute to their love for each other. She would make it special, she vowed silently, a remembrance to be treasured in the years to come.

By the time Joe pulled up in front of the cabin the scene was set and Amber was putting the last touches to the dinner she'd prepared with such painstaking care. Since they'd used up nearly all of their grocery supply it wasn't much in the way of an epicurean delight, but it would have to do.

Adam's ugly table was covered with a heavy damask cloth she'd unearthed in a cupboard, its stark white folds a nice contrast to the two red candles in brass holders waiting to be lighted. Between the candles she'd placed a bowl of freshly picked wildflowers, their multi-hued loveliness lending the table a festive air.

Joe's boots sounded on the porch, his usual brisk pace slowed to a heavier tread. Taking a deep, calming breath, Amber went to the door to greet him. "It's about time you got back, Mr. Morrow," she teased as he walked past her. "Did you get lost?"

His expression gave nothing away as he glanced from the flower-decked table to the flames crackling in the fireplace. "I drove around for a while," he remarked quietly. "I'm sorry I'm late."

It was difficult for Amber to keep a smile on her face when she noticed the deep grooves of tension beside Joe's mouth and the brooding look of depression evident in his dark eyes. Gesturing nervously toward the kitchen, she said with forced cheerfulness, "Since we're leaving in the morning, I thought tonight deserved a special effort from the chef. There's soup à la Campbell's, an omelet fit for a king keeping warm in the oven, and a delicious fruit compote served straight from a beautifully labeled can for dessert. I hope everything meets with your satisfaction, sir."

To her dismay Joe's features seemed to harden before her eyes. "You've gone to a lot of trouble," he muttered gutturally as he moved past her. "Do I have time for a quick shower and a shave?"

"Of course," she replied quietly, hearing the betraying quiver in her voice and turning away before he could see the sheen of sudden tears in her eyes. "I still have to set the table."

Amber had already showered and brushed her hair dry in front of the fire. She'd left it loose the way Joe liked it, and it fell in a silken mass nearly to her waist. She'd chosen to wear one of the casual dresses she'd brought with her, made of a lightweight, uncrushable material in tonings of cream, the bodice appliquéd with pretty golden daisies and green leaves. The neckline was square, and thin spaghetti straps were tied in frivolous bows at her shoulders.

"Amber?"

At the sound of her name she quickly dabbed her eyes with trembling fingers and turned to face Joe. He was standing in the doorway, his mouth curved with gentleness as he whispered, "You look so lovely you take my breath away, baby."

"Thank you, Joe."

A tremulous smile curved her lips, and the expression in her eyes caused Joe to tense with a surge of longing. He wanted to go to her, and yet if he did he knew it would be to plead with her to stay with him. But there was no point in trying to put pressure to bear on Amber, because she'd already left him in no doubt of her decision to resume the life she'd made for herself. A life without him.

With a mumbled apology he turned on his heel, escaping temptation as he strode into the bathroom. But as he showered and shaved he tortured himself with images of her. Amber smiling up at him as she popped a sun-warmed berry into his mouth; Amber indignantly complaining that he wasn't picking his share; Amber laughing up at him as they walked beside the river; Amber with her beautiful emerald eyes slumberous with desire. Amber... Amber... Amber!

Regret was twisting his heart, and there wasn't a damn thing he could do to ease his anguish. Muttering a curse beneath his breath he stormed naked into the bedroom and opened the locks on the single case he'd left behind when he loaded the car. Stepping into clean shorts, he withdrew the denims and blue plaid shirt he'd planned on wearing in the morning.

After he was dressed he returned to the bathroom and pulled on his boots. As he stood to rejoin Amber, he caught sight of his reflection in the mirror. His skin seemed to be stretched too tightly over his cheekbones, his mouth a grim slash, his eyes bleak and empty. Lowering his head, he gripped the edge of the basin with bone-crushing force. For Amber's sake as well as his own he had to maintain control of his emotions, he told himself fiercely—tonight was all they would ever have of each other.

After eating a meal neither of them wanted, Joe and Amber did the dishes. They didn't talk much, because there was nothing left to say. Unspoken between them was the realization of what tomorrow would bring, and neither could face discussing the inevitable. Eventually there were no more tasks to keep them busy; the kitchen was as clean as the rest of the cabin.

All they had to do in the morning was strip the bed, wash and dry the bedding and towels they'd used, fold them into the cedar chest and closet and empty the refrigerator of the few remaining items it held. Not much, Joe thought dourly, but it might keep him sane until he could busy his mind with the mechanics of driving. He only wondered how in hell he was going to handle the minutes and hours and days to come, when memories of Amber would return to torture him.

The buildup of tension between them was almost palpable, and suddenly Joe couldn't take anymore. Searching his mind for a diversion, he asked, "Would you like to leave now, Amber?"

She had preceded him into the living room, but at his question she spun around to face him. "Would you?" she inquired in a tight voice.

"It might be . . . easier," he stated softly. "We're just hanging on until the last minute, and I don't think either of us is gaining anything by dragging this out to the bitter end."

Amber moved forward and slid her arms around his waist, looking up at him with loving eyes. "It needn't be a bitter ending, Joe. Tonight should be a special memory between us, one filled with our love for each other. I'd like to give you that, if you'll let me."

The palm of his hand pressed her head against his chest. "Will you let me give to you in return?"

Amber's silent nod vibrated against his fingers, and Joe's mouth tenderly brushed against her soft, fragrant hair. "We've never made love on the rug in front of the fire," he murmured huskily.

She gave a tearful chuckle and held him even tighter. "We never seemed to get past the couch."

Joe's own laughter was a deep rumble in his chest. "You were always too impatient to ravish me."

Amber jerked her head back until their gazes locked together. "I was always—" She gave him an indignant look, her eyes flashing green fire. "You've always been the one who couldn't wait to..."

He silenced her with his mouth, and when the kiss finally ended she was clinging to him weakly. "You don't play fair," she breathed unsteadily.

Joe was untying her spaghetti straps with nimble fingers. "Do you have anything on under this?" he demanded in choked tones.

Amber clutched at the drooping bodice of her dress, her lashes flickering shyly. "I—I had something special in mind. Will you pour us both a glass of wine while I get ready for you?"

Joe's gaze narrowed with slumberous desire, a dark flush coloring his cheekbones. "You already are special, but I've always liked surprises. To add a subtle warning, though, pressing against me like this isn't going to buy you the time you want."

With a brilliant smile she released him, shooting him a provocative glance over her shoulder as she disappeared in the direction of the bedroom. Joe was still smiling as he uncorked the bottle of champagne they'd bought a week ago and forgotten to drink. He found a battered ice bucket on the top shelf of the cupboard and emptied the last of the ice from the trays in the freezer.

Carrying two crystal wineglasses in one hand and the bucket in the other, he placed them beside the

Navajo rug in readiness for Amber's return. Then he moved to turn out all the lights, the only illumination in the room coming from the cavernous opening of the variegated rock fireplace.

Joe sensed Amber's presence in the doorway, and the hiss of his breath was audible as he looked at her. She was attired in a pale knee-length robe, the front opened to form a plunging neckline, the edges of the collar turned back to expose the white swell of her burgeoning breasts. Her hair was loose and flowing around her shoulders, her feet bare. Guessing that she wore nothing under the robe, he swallowed thickly.

"My God," he groaned almost inaudibly. "You are the most exquisite thing I've ever seen. Come to me, Amber. I think I'm too weak in the knees to move."

With exquisite hesitation Amber walked toward him, her eyes lustrous with emotion. "I love you, Joe."

Her whisper made his body shiver and stirred his soul. He held out his arms in a silent appeal and rasped, "I love you, too."

Nine

Amber evaded Joe's embrace and knelt on the rug, her hand sensuously ruffling the fringed ends as she looked up at him with a pert smile. Patting the place next to her, her voice was huskily beguiling when she inquired, "Aren't you going to sit down?"

Joe lowered himself beside her, mesmerized by the teasing promise in her lovely green eyes. But when he again reached for her, she escaped his circling arms with a light trill of laughter. "Why don't you pour the wine, darling?"

Suppressing a groan of impatience, Joe filled two glasses with the bubbly liquid. His hand shook slightly, and as Amber accepted her drink she acknowledged his tension with a tiny moue of satisfaction. Lifting her glass, she murmured, "I'd like to make a toast. To a special rose, may it bloom tonight and live forever in our hearts."

Both puzzled and intrigued by her toast, he asked, "Are we sharing this rose?"

Amber held his gaze and nodded solemnly. "It belongs to us both, Joe."

They sipped their wine in a silence fraught with anticipation. Joe felt as though the combination of Amber's closeness and the pungent liquid slipping down his throat were igniting a fire in his blood, and when the glass was empty he hurriedly set it aside. Amber placed hers beside it, her gaze intent as she studied his tense features.

"Tonight is a magic time without a beginning or end for us," she said gently. "Have you ever marveled at the perfection of a rosebud, Joe? Each petal is a velvet promise turned in on itself, tightly closed to protect its heart. But if the rose is nurtured, those petals unfurl to become an object of great beauty. You and I together are like that bud, Joe. We closed ourselves off from each other until our love was like broken petals scattered on the winter wind, but now we've been reborn."

Amber caught her lower lip between her teeth, as though hesitating over her next words. Her lashes flickered, but her features held the serene composure of inner faith as she promised, "When we're apart, all we'll have to do to hold on to each other is to wait for spring and watch the roses bloom. I hope there will only be joy and warmth and happiness in the memory. Will you share the magic of our rose with me, Joe?"

Her mouth was glistening moistly from the wine, her eyes radiating a lambent glow as the firelight flickered in their depths. Joe's jaws clenched together to repress the emotion rising within him as without a word he drew her into his arms. "Will you, Joe?" she repeated anxiously, her head cradled against his shoulder as she gazed up at him.

Tenderly he laid her back on the warm rug and began unbuttoning his shirt. When he gave her an encouraging smile, Amber reached up to help him. Her fingers caressed the dark mat covering his chest before moving to his smooth, muscular shoulders. With a muffled cry he leaned over her. "You are my magic, Amber. You are my rose."

Amber brushed aside the black hair which had fallen over his forehead, her face reflecting the intensity of her need. "Love me, Joe."

"Forever," he promised gruffly. "Forever, my love."

Joe leaned unsteadily against the edge of the doorway and stared down sightlessly at the threadbare carpeting beneath his feet. His hair was rumpled, his shirttail hanging half out of his slacks, and his cheekbones carried a gray pallor that heightened the wild glitter in his eyes. When the door in front of him opened a crack, he didn't even bother to look up. "I came to say goodbye," he uttered tonelessly.

The sound of the chain lock being slid open tore through his head with the precision of a hacksaw. Joe staggered when he tried to move past Stella, and her features creased in alarm. Grabbing his arm, she drew it over her shoulders. Half pulling, half carrying him to her couch, she waited until he was slumped against the burgundy and cream throw pillows before finally giving voice to her fears.

"My God," she cried, pulling the ends of her long terry cloth robe over her legs as she sat beside him. "Joe, what's wrong with you?"

He mumbled something indistinguishable and she leaned forward to sniff his breath. "Are you drunk?" she asked suspiciously.

"Migraine," he admitted through gritted teeth, his eyes closing as he leaned his head against the back of the couch. "Going tonight . . . promised you . . . got to leave her . . . my beautiful rose . . ."

Stella smoothed his sweat-beaded forehead with both of her hands. "You're not making any sense, honey. What's happened, what's she done to you?"

"Not enough," he mumbled. "Never . . . enough."

"Joe, open your eyes and look at me!"

Stella's stridently demanding voice made Joe recoil in pain, but it carried enough fear for him to respond to her need for reassurance. Squinting up at her, he attempted a smile. "Not drunk, Stel. S'all right, don't worry."

Her fright escalated at the slurred sound of his speech. "I'm calling my doctor."

Joe gripped her arm when she started to get to her feet. "Pills...in suitcase."

She grasped the garbled information eagerly. "Back at the casino?"

Joe started to shake his head and suddenly gasped, lifting his hands to clutch at his temples. "Car," he muttered harshly.

"Where is it parked?"

But Joe was beyond answering, because this time his eyes were closed in unconsciousness. With a nervous exclamation, Stella searched his pockets for his keys. Then she tore out of her apartment as if the hounds of hell were at her heels, running down three flights of stairs instead of waiting for the elevator. Her robe flapped about her ankles as she exited the building and began searching the parking lot for Joe's car.

It wasn't there, and her sobbing breaths held an edge of frustration. Heading in the direction of the street, she was an incongruous figure as she rounded the corner of the building. Her hair was wound in hot pink rollers and bright red slippers slapped against the pavement as she spotted the black Beretta parked across the well-lighted street. People turned to gape at her, but she was oblivious to their curious stares. Her entire concentration was centered on Joe.

By the time she got back to him, Joe had recovered from his faint and was hunched forward, his elbows braced on his knees and his head held between his hands. Stella hurried past him and entered her small kitchenette, reaching into a cupboard for a glass while she tried to catch her breath. Water sloshed over the edge as she filled the squat tumbler, dripping from her shaking fingers to the floor as she returned to Joe's side.

Stella placed the glass on her coffee table, unconcerned by the ring of moisture marring the wood. She reached into her pocket, carefully reading the directions printed on the small prescription vial she held. Shaking two of the tiny capsules into her palm, she shoved them in the general direction of Joe's mouth. "Here, swallow these."

His hand shook so badly she slipped the medication between his lips and held the glass for him. "What in the world were you doing, driving in this condition?"

Pushing the glass away from his mouth with a grimace, he muttered, "Wasn't that bad when I left."

"Thank God you came here before getting on the freeway," she responded fervently. "You could have killed yourself!"

When he lifted his ravaged face, Stella cringed at the apathetic listlessness of his eyes. "It doesn't matter," he stated bluntly.

"Don't talk like that," she said, her features creased in concern. "You've got everything to live for, Joe."

"Not without Amber," he whispered hoarsely.

With a groan he listed to the side, but Stella caught him before he could fall. She was a small woman, and it took every ounce of her strength to get him into a prone position. Tugging off his boots, she pulled the colorful afghan off the back of the couch and wrapped him in its warm folds. Her blue eyes were filled with pity as she knelt on the rug by his side and listened to him ramble incoherently.

"A sunset rose...so warm, Stel." He twisted his head restlessly and clutched at her sleeve. "Amber...not Carvalho's mistress...believe her...have to believe."

"I believe you," she soothed gently. "Just close your eyes and rest, Joe. You need to rest."

Joe's lashes fluttered down and his mouth convulsed. "Can't rest, Stel. Nothing fits...pieces...all jagged and scattered."

Stella bit her lip at her inability to make any sense of what he was telling her, her cool hand brushing repeatedly over his creased brow. "Everything will be better in the morning. Just sleep now, Joe."

"Didn't sleep last night," he remarked, his voice growing more indistinct. "Held her... last time."

Stella kept brushing her hand over his forehead, and gradually some of the tension began subsiding from Joe's face. She thought the pills had finally taken effect when suddenly he cried out, his entire body tightening with the intensity of his inner turmoil.

"Why?" he asked fiercely. "You love me... making me leave you. What are you hiding? There's something... Carvalho knows... I've got to have answers... the rose... burning me up inside. Have... to trust me... it's so dark. Amber, Amber, please..."

Once he was quiet and breathing evenly, Stella got to her feet and went to the phone. Lifting the receiver she punched out a number and stood listening to it ring. There was a click, and a groggy greeting sounded on the other end of the line.

"Mary Lynn?" Stella said in a voice filled with determination. "Can you meet me at the casino in an hour? I know what time it is, but it's urgent."

Stella tapped her long nails impatiently against the receiver as she waited for her friend's protests to subside. "It's Joe, Mary Lynn. He's out for the count on my couch, and he's been talking crazy."

She listened for a moment, and then replied, "No, he only stopped to say goodbye. I'm frightened for him. He's in a terrible state, and there's got to be something I can do to help him.''

There was a spate of questions from Mary Lynn, and Stella responded worriedly. ''I'll tell you everything when I see you, all right? I'll wait for you in the Cabaret Lounge. Yeah, thanks, honey. I knew you wouldn't let me down.''

Stella replaced the receiver in its cradle and glanced over at Joe. He was deeply asleep, his chest rising and falling in an even rhythm. She hoped he'd sleep until morning, but it didn't really matter. He wouldn't be going anywhere without his keys. Setting her lips with determination, she walked purposefully into her bedroom and began to dress.

Stella sat at one of the tables in the open lounge area behind the bar and watched Mary Lynn's hurried approach. The other woman was out of breath as she plopped into an adjoining chair and apologized for being late. ''You said Joe was talking crazy,'' Mary Lynn reminded her with a frown. ''What's happened to him?''

Stella shook her head, chewing furiously on the gum in her mouth. ''God, it's times like these I wish I still smoked!''

Mary Lynn gave her a warning glare from slitted eyes. ''Will y'all quit chewing and start talking? What in the world is going on?''

Stella explained as well as she could, but when she finished Mary Lynn just gave her a blank look. "He was talking about roses?" she exclaimed incredulously.

"A rose," Stella corrected absently, toying with the keno sheets that were sticking out of a metal holder. "I think it has some connection with Amber, but I'm not certain."

Mary Lynn tapped the edge of her white teeth with a well manicured fingernail. "It doesn't make much sense."

"He wasn't particularly coherent," Stella grimaced, "but one bit of information came through loud and clear, Mary Lynn. According to Joe, Amber isn't Carvalho's mistress."

"I wondered about that," Mary Lynn admitted. "Whenever I've seen them together they didn't act at all like lovers. In fact, just the opposite. There's always been a kind of distance between them, as if they didn't get along particularly well."

"Then Joe was probably right," Stella affirmed with excitement. "He muttered something about Carvalho knowing."

"Knowing what?"

"If I knew that my worries would be over," Stella retorted in irritation. Then a sudden light entered her eyes, and she slammed her hand down on the table with enough force to make her friend jump a foot in the air.

"Don't do that!" Mary Lynn exclaimed, clutching at her chest.

"That's it, don't you see?" Stella cried out triumphantly.

Mary Lynn cupped her chin in her hand, leaning her elbow on the table as she gazed at her with a jaundiced eye. "The only thing obvious to me is that you've just broken your hand."

Stella waved her flexing fingers in the air, and winced. "Forget my stupid hand and listen to me, damn it!"

"I'm all ears," her companion grumbled, managing to yawn and glare at Stella simultaneously. "But if you're going to keep blathering about roses I'm going home."

Stella ignored her complaint, her expression distracted as she said, "Joe also mentioned something about Amber hiding. Don't you get the connection?"

With amazing forbearance considering her confused state of mind, the younger woman asked, "What connection?"

"Amber is hiding something from Joe," Stella replied with gloating certainty, "and Carvalho knows what it is. I'd take bets on it."

Mary Lynn straightened, her eyes widening as she caught some of Stella's enthusiasm. "You could be right."

"Of course I'm right, but the problem is what to do about it."

"You could talk to Mr. Carvalho."

"Not on your life," Stella retorted with a revealing shudder.

"I should have remembered that lurid imagination of yours and never repeated all the gossip that regularly goes the rounds about him." Mary Lynn looked at her in exasperation. "He's really not such a bad guy, Stel. He just isn't very outgoing, that's all."

"Then you talk to him."

Mary Lynn scowled and shook her head. "Oh, no you don't! You're the fanatic in this crowd."

"Please?" Stella wheedled.

"No way," Mary Lynn reiterated. "All he could do is throw you out of his apartment, but I could get fired."

Stella nibbled her lower lip pensively. "That's another problem. From what you've told me, he doesn't allow strangers anywhere near him."

Mary Lynn nodded in agreement and waved her hand in a dismissive gesture. "That's right, but I can get you in to see him."

"You can?" Stella asked. "But don't we need a passkey to go above the twenty-fourth floor?"

"No problem, I'll provide you with a key."

Stella's mouth opened and closed as she stared across the table at Mary Lynn's smug face. "How are you going to manage that?"

"Honey child," Mary Lynn drawled with a snide grin, "don't y'all remember who I've been dating this past couple of months?"

"I'm not privy to your love life," Stella remarked defensively.

Ignoring her friend's ill humor, Mary Lynn gave her a sunny smile. "Ray Pierce, that's who."

This time it was Stella's turn to look blank. "Ray who?"

With a long-suffering sigh Mary Lynn eyed Stella in disgust. "One of Ms. Stevenson's bodyguards. You sure can be dense at times, honey."

"How was I to know who you were dating?" Stella retorted indignantly.

"I introduced you to Ray twice."

Stella flushed at the reminder and grinned sheepishly. "Yeah, now I remember meeting him."

"Anyway," Mary Lynn interjected enthusiastically, "I'm sure if I talk to Ray he'll get you in to see Mr. Carvalho."

"I'm not certain..." Stella's words trailed to a halt under the other woman's derisive stare.

"You're not going to chicken out, are you?"

At the sarcastic accusation, Stella bucked up her courage. "Of course not," she squealed with a marked lack of confidence. "Whatever gave you that idea?"

Mary Lynn's grin was wide and knowing. "Just a hunch, sugar."

"Oh, shut up and call your boyfriend," Stella snapped, glaring her displeasure when her friend had the temerity to laugh at her.

But all too soon Mary Lynn caught the drift of Stella's latest demand, and she stared across the table at her in disbelief. "You want me to call Ray now? It's after midnight, Stel. Some people—at least those without crazy friends like you—do sleep, you know."

"Tomorrow will be too late," Stella replied, letting the comment about her mental well-being slide. "If he hadn't gotten sick, Joe would already be on his way to Los Angeles. As soon as he wakes up he's going to be out of here like a shot."

"Couldn't you talk him into staying for a couple more days? After all, he's the one you're trying to help."

"Too proud," Stella muttered. "I've got the feeling he wouldn't be too happy about what I'm planning to do."

"But knowing you, you'll just plunge in with both feet anyway. All right, I'll do it, but Mr. Carvalho might not be in the best frame of mind for a visitor," Mary Lynn warned.

Stella gulped audibly, her eyes wide with apprehension. "I'll take my chances."

Stella stepped gingerly across the plush gold carpeting, all eyes as she surveyed her surroundings. Openmouthed with wonder, she muttered her appreciation to the man at her side. "This place is a bloody palace. Will you look at those statues? They look like they're pure gold."

"They are," Ray remarked dryly. "The pictures on the walls are Monets, the vase in the corner dates from the Ming dynasty and that collection of jade in the glass cabinet over there is one of the finest in the world. Mr. Carvalho has class."

"Lord! The guy must be richer than a bloody king," she remarked in awestruck tones. "I wonder how he has the time to count all his money?"

"Is that what you came to discuss with me?" a well-modulated voice inquired from the drawing room doorway. Theodore Carvalho approached them, his expression cold. "Aren't you being a little personal, Miss...? I'm afraid Ray just referred to you as a friend of his."

Gasping and almost rigid with nerves, she blurted, "Just call me Stella."

A piercing pair of hazel eyes inspected her from the top of her head to the soles of her feet, and some of the tightness disappeared from his mouth. Gesturing her to a high-backed white damask armchair, he seated himself in its twin. Lifting the lid of a small, heavily embossed casket on the rosewood table set between them, he asked, "Would you care for a cigarette, Ms. . . . Stella?"

Her first attempt at a refusal emerged as a squeak and dark color flowed over her entire face. Trying again, she managed a fairly credible, "No! I mean . . . no, thank you, Mr. Carvalho."

There was a definite twitch to those sternly modeled lips, disappearing in an instant as Theo turned his head to speak quietly to Ray Pierce. Stella was too busy staring to pay much attention to their conversation. She was fascinated by the thin, aesthetic features of the man she'd heard so much about.

Theo Carvalho's gray hair held just a hint of its former color, which appeared to have been a deep russet shade. It was combed severely back from a lined forehead, as though in an attempt to subdue a natural wave. She guessed he was in his late forties or early fifties, but it was difficult to tell. The hands that rested on the arms of his chair were long-fingered with clean, clipped nails. She looked at those elegant hands and shivered, astonished by her reaction. Stella never even noticed when Ray silently left the room.

"Why have you asked to meet with me, Stella?"

Her head jerked up, and she gazed into those heavy lidded eyes without comprehending a thing he'd said. "I . . . I'm sorry, I . . ."

This time his mouth parted in an understanding smile, and Stella gulped at the sight of straight, even white teeth. "You're obviously distressed, but I can assure you that I'm not the villain of your imagination. Now, what did you want to talk to me about?"

Her embarrassment was acute, and she stammered miserably, "I—I'm sorry, Mr. Carvalho. I didn't mean to be rude. It was very thoughtful of you to meet with me at this late hour."

"That's quite all right, my dear. From the impression Ray gave me I assume this is a matter of some urgency?"

It was the kindness in his manner that finally eased Stella's nervousness. With a relieved sigh and an answering smile she relaxed against the comfortably cushioned chair and began to explain her mission of mercy to an intrigued Theodore Carvalho. But as she spoke she noticed his hands tightening against the arms of his chair, and by the time she finished there was a look of incredible sadness in his eyes.

"I see." With a tired sigh he bowed his head and stared down at the carpet, his manner aloof yet oddly vulnerable.

Stella leaned forward, and whispered, "Are you all right, Mr. Carvalho?"

Instead of replying, Theo observed her worried expression with intense concentration. "You have a kind heart, Stella."

Embarrassed by his personal observation, she murmured, "I care about my friends."

"And this man you've told me about," he said, "do you care more about him than your other friends?"

In her usual forthright manner, Stella's reply was openly candid. "The possibility was there in the beginning, but there was never anyone for Joe but Ms. Stevenson. I don't think there ever could be."

His eyes narrowed on her face. "And do you have another . . . special friend?"

Stella's voice shook, her reply a mere whisper of sound as she admitted, "No, Mr. Carvalho."

"Theo," he murmured with a smile. "Call me Theo, my dear. Forgive me for being presumptuous, but I'd like very much to get to know you better."

Stella's eyes were suffused with a radiant light. "I'd like that, Theo."

"No more than I," he responded gently. "I have a great need for kindness in my life, Stella."

Getting to his feet, he held out his hand to her. When she stood beside him, he said, "Why don't you take me to see Mr. Morrow, my dear. I believe there's a great deal I should discuss with that young man."

Ten

Joe pounded on the door in front of him with such ferocity that his knuckles felt bruised. Every thud that reverberated on his eardrums was matched by the angry leap of his pulse. Finally the door was opened a few inches, and he glared at the wan face that appeared in the crack. Her apprehensive upward glance did nothing to ease his temper, and the violent urge he felt to shake her senseless wasn't lessened by the fact that she'd obviously been crying. "Let me in, Amber."

It was purely and simply an order to be followed, but Amber sought to reason with him. "There's no point, Joe. Please, just go away."

"Let me in or I'll break the damned chain!"

Amber saw the febrile glitter in his eyes and knew instantly that further argument was futile. He looked furious enough to break down the door as well as the chain, and with fumbling haste she slid the bolt free. Joe catapulted himself into the room like an avenging angel.

"You little fool," he snarled, slamming the door shut with one hand while he reached for her with the other. "You self-righteous, blind little idiot!"

With scant ceremony she was pulled across the room, her protests going unheeded as he hauled her down beside him on the couch. She was pinned against the cushioned back by his heavy frame, his hands braced beside her reclining head as he demanded, "Why did you hide the truth from me?"

Moistening her dry lips, Amber glanced at him nervously. "I don't know what you're talking about."

"Would it help to refresh your memory if I tell you that I've just spoken with your father?"

Amber went rigid with shock. For a moment the room seemed to spin before resettling in its usual order. But carpet and drapes and lighting fixtures were the least of her concerns as she stared up at Joe, her eyes huge and dilated against the paleness of her face. "You know?" she whispered.

"That Theo Carvalho is your father?" he asked grimly. "Yes. No thanks to you."

Pushing herself out of the confining circle of Joe's arms, Amber rose unsteadily to her feet. Crossing the room, she stood with her back to him as she stared out of the window. Dawn was just tinting the horizon with a brilliant peach-blossom pink, while ghostly wisps of clouds floated across the purple sky. Darkness was rapidly giving way to morning, forced aside by the twilight of a new day.

Amber shivered and drew her teal-blue negligee closer around her body. But the silken folds did little to warm her as her thoughts twisted a tortuous path through her mind. Joe knew everything, she realized, wrapping her arms defensively around her upper torso. "What do you want me to say?" she questioned apathetically.

"I think an explanation is in order, don't you?"

Joe's voice sounded from directly behind her, and Amber had to force herself not to flinch away from his closeness. She could feel the heat of his body melting the chill that surrounded her, but it wasn't a comfort she could accept or give in to. Desperately she sought for some way to avoid a reply, her trembling lips finally forming an accusation. "You had no right going to Theo, Joe. If I had wanted you to know about my relationship with him I would have told you myself."

His returning anger reached out to enfold her only seconds before she was spun around to face him. Hard hands clamped her slender shoulders, while eyes as black as the deepest pits of hell glared at her with sudden comprehension. "You're ashamed," he breathed unsteadily. "You coldhearted little witch, would you deny your own flesh and blood?"

Amber's lips twisted in a mockery of a smile. "Tainted blood—or don't you remember telling me that, Joe?"

His features contorted as he absorbed the painful memory in her eyes, and he closed his own on a wave of regret. "Oh, God!" he rasped harshly. "You must know I didn't mean it that way, baby."

Twisting away from him, she began to restlessly pace the room. "Don't apologize," she snapped impatiently. "I thought the same thing when I was finally told about my illustrious family background."

Joe remained by the window, his gaze intent as he watched her movements. "When did you find out?"

"It seems like a hundred years ago," she responded tiredly. She ran both hands through her hair, pushing it away from her face as though the weight against her temples was too much to bear. "Aunt Cecilia told me the truth just before she died. She didn't want me to think I was all alone in the world."

The glance she sent him was filled with anguished cynicism, while her delicate frame stilled into a defiant stance. "Dear God, she didn't know she was sentencing me to a lifetime of loneliness!"

Joe stared at her in stunned comprehension. "That's why you became cold and distant with me after her death. I put it down to grief, and after you walked out on me I convinced myself you'd changed so drastically because you preferred Theo. Why, Amber?" he groaned in frustration. "Why did you run away without telling me the truth? Didn't you realize that I wouldn't have given a damn?"

The smile she gave him was filled with pained understanding. "But the rest of the world would have, Joe. I knew how much you loved your work and how many ambitions you had to rise in rank. Eventually you would have fulfilled all your dreams, because you're a man who takes hold of them and makes them amount to something. But when that happened there would have been a great deal of publicity, especially regarding your private life. I couldn't live with the fear that some day a clever reporter might ferret out the truth about my past. I couldn't take the risk of destroying your career."

"So you nearly destroyed me instead," he responded heavily.

"No!" she exclaimed in horror. "I didn't mean it to be that way. I was only trying to protect your future, can't you understand that?"

"Oh, I understand," he retorted, approaching her with an angry stride. "It's you who lacks any real understanding of your own motives."

Amber drew away from him until the backs of her legs bumped against the edge of the couch. With a strangled cry she lost her balance, but was caught up in a pair of punishing arms before she had the chance to fall. "You had no right," he raged. "You wrapped your shame around you like a hair shirt, but you made me suffer the pain along with you, Amber."

"That's not true," she gasped. "I . . ."

"Your father loved you enough to deprive himself of the devotion and companionship you would have given him, and instead of being proud of the man for the sacrifice he made you're ashamed."

Amber twisted against his punishing hold, her voice inflected with bitterness as she cried, "Yes, I'm ashamed! I don't know what pretty pictures Theo has painted for you, but the truth is that he just didn't want to bother with me."

Joe grew still. "Is that what your aunt told you?"

Amber stared at the middle button on his shirt, the sound of her breath a painful rasp in the quiet room. "She was too weak to talk for any length of time. I . . . when she gave me the locket she told me it had belonged to her husband, who was a member of my grandfather's organization. When he was killed in a gangland shooting, she left her father's house and never returned. She wanted nothing to do with the Carvalho wealth or name, and when my mother died my father brought me to her to be raised. He provided for us financially, but not once did he come to see the daughter he'd abandoned."

Proudly she lifted her head. "I owe him neither respect nor gratitude," she muttered defensively. "Those two emotions I reserve for my Aunt Cecilia, who gave me her name as well as her devotion."

"Then why did you contact him after she died?"

"I didn't. Aunt Cecilia made arrangements with her lawyer, instructing him to notify her brother through his own lawyers upon the event of her death. When he showed up at the house I didn't even want to let him through the door, but eventually he convinced me we needed to talk."

"What happened then?" he asked.

Amber shrugged with feigned unconcern. "Theo acted the part of the grieving brother and the loving father to perfection, only it came a little late to be truly convincing."

Joe winced at the bitterness in her voice, but he did nothing to distract her train of thought. After a small, significant silence, she continued with her explanation. "I listened politely and asked him to leave, but he made me an offer I couldn't refuse."

At this she began to laugh wildly, while tears flooded her eyes and slipped down her cheeks. "I knew by then I wasn't going to marry you, but I couldn't make myself tell you the reason why. You would have played the quixotic lover to the end, and secretly I was afraid you'd despise me when you knew the truth.''

"How could you have thought that, even for a moment?" he questioned impatiently. "You could have been descended from Attila the Hun for all I cared."

Amber tilted her head back until their eyes met. "You wanted children," she whispered.

Joe frowned. "What in the hell did that have to do with anything. You wanted them, too."

Her throat convulsed as she swallowed, her low tones choked with emotion. "I don't any longer, Joe. The line stops with me."

It took him a moment to catch her meaning, and when he did he stared at her incredulously. "You decided you weren't going to have kids with me or anyone else, and so you settled for a career you didn't want?"

Amber nodded. "That's why I went with Theo even though I despise everything he stands for. It gave me a chance to get away before I dragged you down into the mud with me, Joe. I loved you too much to do that to you, but I never wanted to hurt you the way I did. The note I left was deliberately intended to mislead you about my reasons for running out on you, because I wanted to make a quick, clean break. It was better that way for both of us."

Joe pressed his forehead against hers to hide his reaction to her words. He was stricken at the realization of how needlessly she'd suffered because of him. He knew her aunt had left her the house and a small but adequate monthly annuity in her will. If Amber had never met him she wouldn't have needed to leave her home and her friends. She wouldn't have felt pressured to cut herself free from all she held dear.

He was devastated by the guilt he felt when he remembered the way he had treated her, the terrible things he'd said and done. As if she hadn't been hurt enough, he had deliberately set out to make her pay a penalty she hadn't earned. All her concern had been for him, and he had rewarded her devotion by making her endure his contempt.

"Oh, baby," he groaned. "Can you ever forgive me?"

"Forgive you?" Amber searched his face with troubled eyes. "You haven't done anything to feel guilty for, Joe."

"After the way I treated you, the things I accused you of, you should hate me."

Amber placed the tips of her fingers over his lips and gave him a reproving look. "Our days at the cabin were the most wonderful in my life, and I wouldn't change one moment we spent together."

Joe's lips twisted with remorse. "I would make a new beginning for you, but you're right when you say our time together was wonderful. It was in our Eden that I discovered my beautiful amber rose."

With a choked cry she threw her arms around his neck, and nestled her head beneath his chin. "That's the way I want you to remember me, Joe."

"I won't have any difficulty, since you're going to be with me for the rest of my life."

"That's not possible," she responded dully. "Nothing has happened to change my mind."

"Then I'll have to change it for you," he murmured, his mouth nuzzling the soft skin beneath her ear.

"Don't you understand?" she cried. "I'm still the granddaughter of Sebastian Carvalho."

"But you are also the daughter of Theodore Carvalho, a man who has spent his entire life trying to atone for his father's sins, my darling."

Sliding her hands over his shoulders, Amber pulled away from the soft seduction of his mouth. Blinking the moisture from her eyes, she studied him in confusion. "I don't understand."

"Your father's wealth has been earned through honest labor and careful investments. His father's ill-gotten gains have been spent on various hospitals and charities, but under an assumed name. He wanted no publicity, because he's no more anxious to stir up the past than you are, honey. From what I gather, he and your aunt suffered too much trauma in their youth to relish being in the public eye."

"I don't believe you," she stated coldly. "If that's true, then why didn't he tell me?"

"He didn't think you'd believe him."

Amber flushed at the rebuke implicit in Joe's statement but continued stubbornly. "He could have shown me records, bank statements, anything to substantiate his claim."

"Remember how you described a rosebud, the petals all closed inward?" When she nodded, he remarked, "Theo is like you in many ways—sensitive, caring, but too afraid of opening up for fear he'll expose his vulnerability. You made no secret of your contempt for him, and he's too used to that attitude in others to fight against it."

"He wouldn't have had to if he'd kept me with him, Joe!"

Joe heard the cry of the abandoned child, and his features softened with love and understanding. "No, but in those days his father was still alive and he feared the hatred of the Carvalho name from rival factions would take you as they had your mother."

"My mother?" she questioned on a gasping breath. "She died in a car accident. That's what Theo himself told me."

"Because he couldn't bear you to know the truth, honey. He hired the best bodyguards in the business to protect you from harm, but he didn't want you to live in constant fear the way he's had to for most of his life."

Amber began to tremble, her voice weak and thready as she asked, "How did my mother die?"

"Enemies of your grandfather's were determined to take revenge on the old man by depriving him of his only son. They rigged a bomb in Theo's car, only it was your mother who turned the key in the ignition."

Amber swayed, her lips nearly bloodless as she tightened them against the horrible truth. Joe supported her weight, his body giving her the strength she needed to absorb the shock of what she'd just heard. "Why didn't he tell me, explain that he was trying to keep me safe? It would have breached so many misunderstandings between us."

"My guess is that he blamed himself for your mother's death."

Amber showed her bewilderment by the brief shake of her head. "It wasn't his fault."

"But he was born a Carvalho, with all the stigma the name implied." Joe's eyes were darkly intent as he held her gaze. "Like his daughter, he felt guilt and shame that shouldn't have been carried on his shoulders."

"And also like his daughter," she murmured in acute distress, "he chose to hide himself away rather than face the world with pride and dignity."

Joe nodded, then added quietly, "You and Theo seem to think alike about the things that matter, honey. He, too, was willing to sacrifice himself to protect the one person he loved most in the world."

"Oh, Joe," she whispered, "how my hostile attitude must have hurt him."

"Maybe, but he brought a great deal of your anger on his own head, Amber. He should have been honest with you from the beginning, but he was too proud to admit how much he needs you. It was that damnable pride that kept him from reaching you on an emotional level, and he deeply regrets his inability to communicate. To do so he would have had to reveal the real cause of your mother's death, and he was afraid he would lose you completely if you knew the truth."

While he was speaking Joe slid his arms around her waist, and now his hands were moving in soothing strokes up and down her back. But it wasn't enough to dispel her tension, and with a growl of impatience he sat down on the couch and pulled her onto his lap. "There," he murmured in satisfied tones, "isn't that better?"

One of Amber's arms was caught between their bodies, and the other pushed ineffectively against his chest. "Let me go."

Joe ignored her demand, instead brushing his mouth from side to side against her temple. "I don't want to."

"You sound like a thwarted child," she muttered weakly, her pulse pounding furiously against the warm coercion of his lips.

A husky laugh rumbled from deep in his chest. "Keep wriggling around like that and you'll soon be able to feel how much of a child I am."

Amber froze instantly, a delicate flush staining her cheeks. Looking up at him pleadingly, she said, "This isn't getting us anywhere."

His grin held wicked enjoyment. "That's a matter of opinion."

"Not as far as I'm concerned."

Her stubbornness didn't faze him. He lowered his head until his hoarse whisper feathered across her mouth. "You're not moving an inch until you promise to marry me, my love."

Joe's brand of persuasion was a sensual assault that Amber was powerless to deny. His tongue stroked against her lips until they parted for him, a deep groan of approval matching the increasing intimacy of his kiss. Slowly her hand rose to stroke the back of his neck, while her toes curled inside her fluffy white slippers.

But when his fingers parted the loose folds of her robe, Amber's mind awoke to the danger of weakening from her purpose. Nothing had changed and nothing ever would. She was still the granddaughter of a gangland leader, and even if she could accept that her father wasn't tarred by the same brush, Joe could still be hurt by his association with her.

Amber tried to still the hand that was moving upward in search of a high, rounded breast. "I won't marry you, Joe."

Joe gave her a knowing grin, his thumb flicking against a taut nipple. "Yes you will."

Totally out of patience with his stubborn refusal to see sense, she muttered, "I will not be responsible for destroying your career!"

"To hell with my career," he countered happily, his mouth beginning to roam over the white flesh he'd uncovered.

Amber arched her back to facilitate his tongue, which had begun to lave the hardened tip until it grew almost painfully tight. "I . . . oh, Joe!"

She was completely distracted for an instant, but eventually responded to his earlier statement. "You really mean it, don't you?"

"I'll take my promotion to detective status because I won't want to work undercover any longer, and during the celebration dinner they'll give me to announce my appointment, I'll be proud to introduce my father-in-law myself."

Joe gave her a smug look before resuming his task. "We'll be married tomorrow," he informed her firmly. "Theo and Stella are making all the arrangements."

After a brief tussle, Amber managed to free her trapped arm. Taking his face in her hands, she reluctantly pulled him away from the object of his interest. "Theo and who?" she asked faintly.

"My friend Stella," he remarked with a grin. "She's the one who dragged your father over to her apartment to meet me. Boy, was I surprised when I woke up to see him sitting there watching me."

"Joseph Morrow, just what were you doing in that apartment in the first place?"

"I went to say goodbye and arrived with a head that felt like King Kong had trounced it. I guess my lucky leprechaun was sitting on my shoulder, or I'd be on my way home by now."

"He was probably the one hitting you on the head with a hammer, and if you don't tell me the rest I'm going to take a leaf out of his book."

Joe didn't look in the least repentant. "Stella shoved two of my pills down my throat and I went out like a light."

"Where?" she asked suspiciously.

With wide-eyed innocence, he replied, "In her apartment."

Gritting her teeth, Amber gave him the haughtiest look she could manage considering her ignominious position on his lap. "Where in her apartment?"

Joe wagged a reproving finger under her nose. "On the couch, and has anyone ever told you that you have a suspicious mind?"

Amber bit the offending appendage, and when he yelped she looked extremely satisfied. "Get on with your story."

Checking his finger for any permanent damage, Joe returned it and the rest of his hand to her breast. Amber was so intent on the pleasurable sensations coursing through her body that she almost missed his next words. But eventually they penetrated the sensual fog clouding her brain, and she gasped. "What did you say?"

"I said there's nothing much to tell," he remarked innocently. "Stella went to talk to Theo while I was out for the count, and she brought him back to her apartment."

"Not that part," she retorted, accompanying her words with a low moan as his hand slid over her smooth thighs.

"Not that part?" He lifted his hand, and chuckled huskily when she glared at him and guided it back in place.

"You know very well what I mean!"

"Oh! I only said that Theo and Stella looked pretty chummy when I left. I offered him a ride, but I don't think he heard me."

"And?" she questioned warningly.

"And would you mind a young stepmother?"

"That's what I thought you said," she breathed wonderingly. "Oh, Joe, do you really think . . . ?"

"I don't want to think," he groaned. "Just tell me you'll marry me before I blow a gasket."

Amber gave him a look of such pure joy that Joe's heart faltered briefly before picking up speed. "Yes," she murmured against his warm, hungry mouth. "Oh, yes, Joe!"

Without further delay he jumped to his feet with her in his arms and carried her into the bedroom. With slow enjoyment he deprived her of her robe and gown and laid her against the deep rose comforter. Then he tore the clothes from his own body, his impatience driving him mercilessly.

Joe bent over Amber, muttering her name as he trailed fiery kisses from her mouth to the soles of her feet. He lingered a long time on her breasts, suckling the nipples until she cried out with pleasure. Then the soft swell of her stomach demanded his attention, and Amber moaned and arched against him restlessly. His hands stilled her writhing body, stroking her thighs apart until deep tremors of need shuddered through her.

"I love you, Joe!"

He smiled against her thigh, no longer needing to be convinced of Amber's love for him. His pulse thudded a primitive beat as he slid his hands down her sides until he gripped her hips. He muttered words of love thickly beneath his breath, and Amber responded by opening herself to his slow, sweet invasion of her body. His mouth reached for succor, his lips teasing hers with tantalizing kisses.

When he started to move with rhythmic urgency, Amber's long, slim legs wrapped around his waist to hold him tightly. It was a ritual dance of giving and taking, with no twilight shadows to mar the paradise they'd found together. As the two lovers cried out with the fierceness of their release, they reached together for the rose. It was in full bloom, a thing of beauty too exquisite for words.

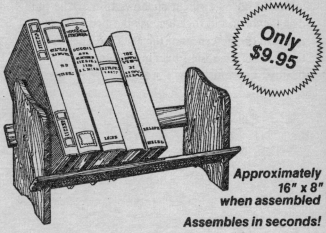

Silhouette Desire®

1989
IS THE YEAR
OF THE MAN!

What makes a romance? A special man, of course, and Silhouette Desire celebrates that fact with *twelve* of them! From Mr. January to Mr. December, every month spotlights the Silhouette Desire hero—our **MAN OF THE MONTH**.

Sexy, macho, charming, irritating…irresistible! Nothing can stop these men from sweeping you away. Created by some of your favorite authors, each man is custom-made for pleasure—*reading* pleasure—so don't miss a single one.

Diana Palmer kicks off the new year, and you can look forward to magnificent men from **Joan Hohl, Jennifer Greene** and many, many more. So get out there and find your man!

Silhouette Desire's

MAN OF THE MONTH …

MAND-1